LEGACY OF A LAND HOG

JOHN REESE

DOUBLEDAY & COMPANY, INC.
GARDEN CITY, NEW YORK
1979

All of the characters in this book are fictitious,
and any resemblance to actual persons, living or dead,
is purely coincidental.

First Edition

ISBN: 0-385-14727-9
Library of Congress Catalog Card Number 78–68347
Copyright © 1979 by John Reese
All Rights Reserved
Printed in the United States of America

Dedicated to Chris Tucker,
good worker, good friend,
and reader of excellent
editorial taste.

LEGACY OF A
LAND HOG

CHAPTER 1

Thirty strong they rode, a small army because Uncle Frank McNeil had to have more of everything than anybody. Half a length in the lead, holding the pace to a slow canter that would not kill a horse in this heat, rode Terence McNeil, who was not so Irish as he sounded. His mother was Italian, and his maternal grandmother, he had heard, was English.

He was twenty-three years old, slim, wiry, and with a good-looking face that was perhaps too expressive of his thoughts, just as his thoughts were too sensitive for a huge cow ranch. He was obeying orders in keeping the lead because Uncle Frank said that when you ran an outfit, you led it. He had little interest in either running or leading a cow crew, but now it was a way station in life that at least was new and different.

To his right, and half a horse's length behind, rode old Pete Viscaino. He liked and trusted Pete more than any man he knew here in this quarrelsome outfit. He caught a warning look from Pete and turned to look to his left, where Baron Godfrey was letting his horse stretch itself a little as they neared home.

At least a dozen assorted dogs lolloped along around and behind the horses. At least another dozen would be awaiting them at home. Uncle Frank could not part with a dog and he let them multiply freely so long as they could feed themselves by hunting. Cats, too, although he would not

allow one in the house. Cats were forever slinking or streaking under your feet, but they kept the ranch rat-free and
gopher-free, and they earned their keep.

The wagon that hauled the fencing tools, drawn by two
teams, was half a mile behind. Baron, a lean and shaggy
man with the countenance of a tame wolf—to be trusted
only in a muzzle and on a chain—had let his horse gain still
more as Terence looked back. It was done with a purpose,
to see how far Baron could go, and the answer had to be
quick and firm.

"Baron!" he called sharply. "Let's hold it down. No use
wearing a horse out for nothing."

Godfrey turned in the saddle and leaned his weight on
one hand behind the saddle. "Sooner we get out of this
sun, the better I'm pleased," he said, "and the better my
horse is pleased, too."

"Well, I'm not pleased, and I say hold him in."

Baron squinted at him, still testing him. "I don't know
as I need anybody to tell me how to ride a horse, sonny."

"Suppose you tail us in today. Drop back behind, Baron.
That's an order, and if you want to argue about it, write
me from Texas."

That's where Baron claimed to come from. His sun-
burned face hardened. It was not a very intelligent-looking
face, but there was something tough and knowing and bitterly wise in it. Terence had often caught this expression
on Godfrey's face and had thought it was the look you'd
see on a chained wolf if you beat him over the head long
enough. Eventually you could trust him not to tear your
arm off—most of the time.

Most of these men wore guns, Baron Godfrey among
them. A gun was a working tool, like the fence pliers most
carried on their saddles or the livestock knives in their

pockets. Terence did not wear a gun, and he did wear gloves.

"What do you mean, 'tail us in'?" Baron asked.

"I mean follow the work wagon, make sure he doesn't drop anything off and lose it, help him if he needs help, and then help unload him."

Godfrey turned and cantered his horse back to follow the wagon without a word. Terence glanced at Pete Viscaino and caught the hint of a smile that said he had handled Godfrey right.

Terence would not have cared whether his uncle liked it or not, but Pete's approval meant something to him, and he did not understand why. Pete had no enemies, but no intimate friends either. Everyone respected him, and that seemed to suffice him.

"Lord*ee*, it's hot," somebody said.

"Don't do no good to complain," another said. "If old Frank can't do nothing about it, as close to God as he is, nobody can."

"I'll speak to Uncle Frank about it," Terence said. "See if I can't get him to put in a word."

"Talk to your Uncle Ernest and Aunt Julia, too, while you're at it."

He laughed. "If they put in a word, God would only ask Uncle Frank, 'How about it; is that what you want done?'"

They turned up the foothills to where a small grove of eucalyptus trees, planted, some said, by the mission fathers fifty years ago, were now towering giants that sheltered what was more of a town than a ranch. From here old Frank McNeil ran the property he had spent thirty years acquiring: the Viscaino place. The Mitchell place. Barr and Robertson's old Possum Track. The ten thousand acres he had diddled a rich mining company out of; they had paid a dollar an acre, but Uncle Frank had persuaded them that it had no minerals and had bought it for a hundred dollars. And of course all the Méxican claims and grants: Martínez, Vegas, Camacho, de la Cruz, God knew who else.

The closer you got to it, the bigger it looked, with the two-story main house squatting among a grove of pepper trees. The old man loved those pepper trees. Like olive trees, they lived forever, as he seemed to be planning to do.

The house was built of logs, but Uncle Frank had had it sided with redwood boards and battens in front, had had bigger windows put in, and a long, roofed *pórtico* built along the entire front. The old roof of redwood slabs had been covered with rounded mission tile. Two round flower beds, edged with brick, adorned the dry front yard and were hand-watered daily by the Méxicans, but he still would not fence the house, and long-legged game chickens wandered the yard and *pórtico* freely. The women were continuously cleaning up after them.

Uncle Frank must have heard them coming because he suddenly appeared at the door. María had to help him over the doorsill, but now he shook off her hand and waved to Terence: *Come here!* He did not use a cane, and he sat down in his cowhide rocking chair without help.

"Will you look at that? Ninety-four and the old son of a bitch is still going strong," one of the men said admiringly.

Terence waved and called, "In a few minutes, Uncle Frank."

Frank's younger brother—Uncle Ernest was a mere eighty-eight—came out, too, leaning on a cane, to watch the big crew sweep around the house and head for the buildings and corrals behind it. They were in the lowest foothills of the Sierra Nevada, northeast of Merced. To the west stretched endlessly the profligately rich Central Valley, and Uncle Frank's west line was five miles away. The upward slope to the east was fine cattle range, and some of it had good merchant timber on it, too. And beyond that, hidden in heat haze today, rose the peaks of the tallest mountains in the continental United States.

As far as the old man could see in all four directions, he owned everything in fee simple. Not only did he not owe a cent to anybody; only his lawyer had any idea how much he held in the way of bank stock, railway bonds, and other gilt-edged securities. He kept them in a big iron safe in his second-story bedroom, with heavy timbers set like posts beneath it to carry the weight. In the downstairs living room the posts had been utilized to hold cranes for lamps and flowers and shelves for bric-a-brac.

Behind the house the old man's Dot M Dot was divided, really, into three distinct entities. You could just see the roof of the Viscaino place a mile to the north. Once there had been a town here by that name, started by the Viscainos, the first Portuguese to settle in this part of California. They had owned their land free and clear, too, but they were not ranchers. They wanted to raise sweet-wine grapes, and Pete's father had made the mistake of borrowing money from old Frank McNeil to fence and plant.

Their money ran out before they planted a single grape. When Frank foreclosed, he did so in the kindliest manner. He promised to leave the Viscainos the property in his will, having no children of his own. Now the only Viscainos left were Pete and his wife, Renata. Their three grown sons, Marco, Patricio, and Angelo, refused to live here as beggarly heirs. They were all in their thirties now, working in lumber camps and on cow ranches and visiting their parents only when it could be done without staying overnight.

Marco, Patricio, and Angelo were not the only people

who felt that way about old Frank McNeil. His own
brother and sister did, too. Only Pete Viscaino had the
guts to talk up to the old man, and he got away with it
only because Frank had seen him grow up from boyhood,
and he could not part with anything that represented the
past.

"Goddamn it, Pete," he had exploded once, "you got a
hell of a lot of guts to distrust me, a goddamn immigrant
like you. I was born in New Jersey when Washington was
still President. My father lived to be a hundred, and so will
I. Ernest, he was born under Adams, the old pinch-nose
son of a bitch. Julia was born under Jefferson."

"I still don't trust you worth a damn, Frank," said Pete.

Frank did not even hear him. "Funny that the youngest
one was the first to die. He was my half brother, James,
born to my father's second wife. Terence's father, born
when James, the old goat, was fifty-eight. He'd be—let's see
—eighty-one if he was alive today. He married a goddamn
Italian singer thirty years younger than him. President of
the Gold Star Steamship Lines, but when he died, he
didn't leave as much as I owned at the time. President of a
company, what the hell kind of job was that?"

. . . . . You never knew whether his mind was wandering or he was putting on an act. Pete could be philosophical about living in the house his father had built,
surrounded by Dot M Dot range. But Terence knew that
it hurt him, deep in his guts, a hurt that never went away.

Between Pete's place and the main ranch buildings was
the *barrio* where the Méxicans lived. A Méxican got paid
the same as an American if he could do the work. Single
ones sometimes lived in the big bunkhouse. Old Frank was
patrón to up to a hundred of them. He spoke bad Spanish
fluently and saw to it that widows and orphans kept their
houses and drew their rations without payment.

And then there were the big haybarn and the surrounding corrals, in three of which fine hot-blood stallions were kept. The bunkhouse, which slept up to forty men, and its kitchen and dining room, which fed as many, were spotless. Frank raised more hell about an untidy bunkhouse than he did about taxes.

There were five windmills pumping water from deep, drilled wells here behind the house. Terence began trembling with eagerness as they rode over a low slope and the one that watered the Méxican village came into sight.

Hanging from the frame of the mill was a signal, a gourd dipper of green and red. He told the men to knock off for the day and he'd fix it up with Uncle Frank. The men headed for the corrals with a whoop, all but Pete Viscaino, who nodded his thanks and turned in the other direction toward his house.

Terence stripped the saddle and bridle from his horse and turned it into the corral. He went to the windmill, filled the gourd dipper, and drank from it with hands that still trembled as they held it. He diverted the outflow pipe long enough to wash the dust from his face, hands, and arms. He started toward the Méxican houses, carrying the gourd.

"The old man waved for you to come in," Baron Godfrey called. He was on his way to the house himself, to report to Uncle Ernest. He was a sneak and a spy, but he was the least of Terence's worries.

"I'll be along shortly."

Terence carried the dipper to the small, neat redwood house surrounded by flowers and vegetable rows, a little aside from the others. He went around it to the back door, tapped on it twice, and then twice again.

A chain rattled inside. He pushed the door open, and there stood Eloísa Sánchez, eighteen years old, tawny of

skin, ethereally beautiful, and stark naked. The glowing
smile on her face showed him how she loved to surprise
him this way.

He tossed the dipper on a table and reached behind him
to chain the door. He enfolded her in his arms and felt her
go limp.

"I thought you would never come, my wonderful man,"
she crooned as he began to caress her. "Hurry, my beloved.
Hurry—love me, love me, love me!"

"What if your mother comes back?" he choked.

"She will give us plenty of time. She put flowers in a vase
beside the bed. Don't waste our time, my beautiful man.
Love me, love me, love me!"

She spoke perfect English, and there was some American
blood in her somewhere. He picked her up in his arms and
carried her to her tiny bedroom as she unbuttoned his
shirt. Sure enough, María had filled a big glass vase with
fresh flowers and put it on a round table near the bed, and
someone had turned back the coverlet. He put her on the
bed, a lustrous smile illuminating the beauty of her face.

They had blundered into this blindly, and she was a
skilled as well as passionate mate. At least twice a week
they did this, sometimes by night but more often by day.
They had become so good at it that it seemed to fill them
both with something like glory.

He feasted hungrily. In a moment she pushed him away.
"Your uncle wants you," she said, "but I knew you'd come
to me first. Now go, before you get us both in trouble."

He stood up and took up the towel that lay folded beside the vase; he dried off the sweat and smiled at her. "I
love you," he said.

"I know you do," she said sleepily, "and I love you, too.
Better go now."

He left her satiated and damp on the bed. He leaned

over to kiss her eyes before slipping out and closing first her
bedroom door and then the back door behind him. Every
such parting filled her with sorrow, and they were beginning to sadden him, too. He had made love to many
women, for all his youth, but none had ever stirred in him
this mystical sweetness in which there was always a touch
of sadness.

He had been here long enough to know how the
Méxicans felt about such things. To be the beloved of the
nephew of the señor was honor enough, was to be expected
if a girl was both beautiful and lucky. The subject of marriage had never come up, and he knew somehow that his
uncle would raise hell if it did. And because he did not in-
tend to spend the rest of his life as a guest of an uncle he
had never known on a cattle ranch that had never held any
temptation for him, he was not quite sure how he felt. Almost, but not quite.

He walked down to the house and went in through the
kitchen door. The kitchen women knew where he had
been, but they ignored him. Old Uncle Ernest, who disliked Terence almost as much as Terence disliked him,
heard him coming and shuffled in from the dining room
pantry, leaning on his cane. He was a bigger man than
Uncle Frank and fat and untidy, for all his fine clothes.

"I told Baron I wanted him to eat dinner with us. Now
Frank says it's up to you," he said. "Hell of a note if I have
to ask you. Who the hell do you think you are around here,
anyway?"

"Just see that he washes his dirty neck," Terence said.
"Where is Uncle Frank?"

"At the table in the tea room. He and Julia have been
waiting for you. I wouldn't, believe me!"

"Calm down before you have a heart attack," Terence
said. "Come on, let's go eat."

CHAPTER 2

The tea room had been so named by Aunt Julia, the widow
of Phineas Orr. It was leftover space that once had served
as an office for Uncle Frank and was as unhandy for the
servants as possible. Everything had to be brought from the
kitchen through the pantry and the long dining room, and
once Julia had bought a bell with which the summon the
servants. Frank had promptly confiscated it for use in his
bedroom.

Phineas Orr had left Julia a little money, but he had
died thirty years ago, and it had all run out. Like Uncle
Ernest, she was completely dependent on her eldest
brother. Like him, she hated the ranch and could not understand why Frank did not give them an allowance so
they could live in the east or at least in San Francisco. And
like Ernest, she suspected Terence of conniving to inherit
Frank's property and detested him.

The tea room was so small that one end of the table was
against a wall. For years Julia had sat at Frank's right. She
still tried to sit there occasionally now and had seated herself there today.

Frank had the head of the table. He grinned at Terence
as he came into the room but ignored Ernest. "Come sit
beside me, boy," he said. "Julia would rather have her own
place anyway, and I want to talk to you."

Julia stood up and moved as far from Terence as possible. Ernest sat down across from them, facing Terence, and

in a moment Baron Godfrey came in and sat down opposite Julia, giving her a little bow. He was trying to learn.

"I notice the horses all look good," Frank said to
Terence. "Me and Miguel took a little walk around this
morning. Never saw them in better shape. You're a good
hand with a horse, my boy."

"I did two years in a military college, you know,"
Terence said. "I sat up many a night with a sick horse, and
I learned pretty well how to keep them from getting sick."

"One of the brown horses on the yard wagon stumbles
now and then," said Baron.

"You'd stumble, too, if you was his age. That's old Rex.
He's almost thirty. You figure seven years of a man's age to
one of a horse, and he's the equal of a man two hundred
and ten years old," Frank said.

"He ought to be put out of his misery."

"He ain't miserable."

María, Eloísa's mother, came in with a big tureen of
chicken soup. She was a small woman, chunky rather than
chubby, grave of manner, sure of herself and her position
here, and totally dedicated to her daughter's welfare.
Strangers were often confused that she could be María
González and her daughter Eloísa Sánchez. When a
Méxican woman married, she retained her maiden name,
merely adding her husband's, so that while Eloísa's father
lived, she was María González de Sánchez. If María's
dream came true and Eloísa married Terence, she would be
known, among the Méxicans at least, as Eloísa Sánchez de
McNeil. She served Frank first, then Julia, Terence, Ernest,
and Baron in order. After the soup there was a salad, at
which Frank made a face. He ate a few bites and then put
his fork down.

"Somehow I ain't hungry," he said.

"It's all that rock candy you ate this morning," Julia said. "I warned you. You need your greens."

"I need a nap. Maybe Terence will help me up to my room and then come up and talk to me after he's done eating."

There was silence while María and Terence helped the old man to his feet. He took Terence's arm and let himself be guided to the wide stairs at the back of the house. Terence heard a horse in the yard—it sounded like a buggy to him—and said so.

"It's Foster Bainbridge," Frank said. "I forgot about him. You tell him to come up to my room after he eats."

Bainbridge was Frank's lawyer. Terence had met him and liked him. He helped the old man sit down in the big rocking chair and got a stool for his feet before going down. María had already set a fresh plate at Frank's place for the lawyer.

"Hello, Terence," Bainbridge said. "You're looking very fit. Ranch work agrees with you."

"You ought to try a little of it yourself," said Terence. You're putting on a little weight, aren't you?"

Bainbridge was about fifty, but he did not look it. He patted his stomach and said, "I've got a good gusset maker. Lady who mends and does laundry and so forth. As long as she can make my pants fit, I'll avoid all unnecessary exercise. How's Frank?"

"Tiptop," said Terence.

"He needs more sleep," Julia said, "and Terence keeps him up all night, talking with him and playing that scratchy violin until nobody in the house can sleep."

"Now, Julia, an older person doesn't need as much sleep as a young one. You know that."

"I know nothing of the kind! He needs proper food, too, but he just snacks."

"There his doctor is against you. He says that spacing out his sleep in deep naps and spacing his meals out in nourishing snacks so he never puts too great a strain on his body will extend his life for years."

"Dr. Payne said that?" Julia cried.

"Yes. We have discussed it many times."

"I wonder about the propriety of that, Mr. Bainbridge," said Ernest.

"I suggest you discuss it with him yourself. A man of ninety-four is a special medical problem, and Dr. Payne has had similar experience with other patients. Frank is in excellent health."

There was a moment of silence. Ernest blurted, "Is he changing his will? You've been out here, and he's been in to see you. We have a right to know why."

"Now, Ernest, you know better than that," the lawyer said patiently. "I can only tell you what Frank said I should tell you last month: that he is providing for both of you."

"He won't even discuss it with us," said Julia.

Bainbridge shrugged. "I can't help that, and I can't interfere, Julia."

"But the man is getting feeble-minded. He is not competent to make a will," Ernest said.

"I assure you that he could pass every test for competency, Ernest."

María brought in a platter of fried chicken. One of the other women brought a bowl of boiled potatoes and a bowl of gravy. Ernest looked at them with distaste and turned to Baron Godfrey.

"Baron, I believe I could stand a drink of rum, if you will be so obliging."

"Sure." Baron got up and went into the dining room to

the sideboard. He brought back a half-gallon bottle and a big tumbler. "Say when," he said, and began pouring.

"Stop, stop!" Ernest cried.

Godfrey put the glass down in front of him, but Ernest's hand was too unsteady to pick it up. Godfrey held it while he sipped several healthy gulps of rum. Some of it dribbled down his chin as he tried to pull away from the glass, which Godfrey kept pressed to his mouth.

Terence shot to his feet. "That's enough, Baron," he said sharply. "That's all he wants; that's all that's good for him. Put the glass down."

Godfrey narrowed his wolf's eyes and put the glass down. Ernest seemed about to strangle on the rum, but in a moment he caught his breath. Terence pointed to the .45 that swung at Godfrey's hip.

"Don't wear that thing to the table again, Baron," he said. "Don't wear it into this house."

Godfrey stared at him insolently. "I've always gone armed. That's why I'm alive today."

"You heard me. Either remove your gun before you come into this house, or stay out."

Ernest had his breath back. "You have no right to talk to Baron that way. You do not give the orders here. Not in the house, you don't."

"All right, I'll speak to Uncle Frank, and I'll tell him I think we can get along without Baron altogether."

"Oh no, don't do that! You can't have a man fired for so trivial a thing."

"Let us have peace," Julia pleaded. "Mr. Godfrey, you can surely take your gun off safely in my brother's house. It *is* an uncouth habit, to me at least."

"Sure!" Godfrey unbuckled his holster, wrapped it around the gun, and put it on the floor. He took his place at the table again. All began eating, but Terence and Bainbridge were the only ones to attempt to carry on a conversation. The two old people gobbled their food untidily and scowled at their plates until Terence excused himself to do his evening chores.

Terence had not known much about his family. He knew that his father was the son of his grandfather's middle age, by a second marriage, and that he himself had some aged uncles and aunts somewhere. His mother had not known the McNeils at all.

James McNeil died when Terence was twelve, leaving a comfortable, if not lavish, estate. It was enough to keep him in military school and at years of study of the violin. Eventually he decided that, like his mother's operatic voice, his talent was not quite first-rate even at its best, and sometimes was downright bad.

The money could keep his mother comfortably, but it could not keep him in idleness, too. It was his mother's idea that he visit his relatives in California and renew family ties. "Go see your Uncle Frank," she had said. "He's very rich; I know that for a fact. Surely he will want to find something congenial for you to do."

Terence had put it off as long as he could. The idea of sponging off an aged relative he had never met repelled him, but his mother kept after him until at last he wrote to Uncle Frank. In reply he had received an affectionate invitation to come and stay as long as he liked and a draft for five hundred dollars to cover his expenses.

He had liked Uncle Frank immediately, but he could not make himself like Uncle Ernest and Aunt Julia. He knew they suspected that he was trying to worm his way into a share of the old man's estate. There was so much ill will in the house that he had planned on cutting his visit short after a week.

A long talk with Foster Bainbridge and Dr. Harry Payne had changed his mind. It was, they said, his duty to make the old man's last years as pleasant as he could.

"Frank is by no means childish," Dr. Payne said. "Bull-headed, old-fashioned, stubborn as a mule—yes. But those are not the clues to a failing mind. Those two make him miserable and he hasn't a friend in the county except us."

"How about Pete Viscaino?"

"Pete isn't his friend. Pete is a remarkably patient and forgiving man. Your uncle is what we call a range hog out here. He has obtained his land by strictly legal means, true enough, but Pete is one who went to him for a loan and found that Frank only wanted his land. It's that way with everyone. Only the Méxicans like and trust him because he has always taken care of them, protecting them against people who would have taken advantage of them."

"Let's have one thing understood," Terence said. "I don't want his money. I don't like ranch life, and by now, I'm not sure I like Uncle Frank."

Bainbridge said, "He's not that bad. Frank is a product of his times, and they were very tough times, very long ago. He came out here during the gold rush and made his first fortune buying range beef and driving it up to the gold camps to butcher. He's so tough a man in a deal that it's a form of genius, but these bloodsuckers don't care how he got the money, just so he passes it on to them. Stay with him!"

"I'll think about it."

Terence never did decide to stay. He merely kept postponing his departure, mostly because Ernest and Julia kept nagging him about it. Their terror grew daily as the old

man became fonder and fonder of Terence and more dependent on him.

It was Baron Godfrey who made up his mind, if it could
be said to be made up. Terence had disliked Baron from
the first. His discovery that Ernest was paying Baron little
sums to report Terence's daily doings firmed up Terence's
resolution to stay from day to day. That—and Eloísa
Sánchez.

It would be hard to leave Eloísa now. Someday he had
to talk to his uncle about her, but that was something he
kept putting off from day to day, too. He was the creature
of his own indecision. No two people as different as Eloísa
and Baron could be imagined, but they rather than Frank
McNeil and all his money kept him here.

CHAPTER 3

No more than seven or eight miles south of the McNeil place lay a dying town called Scobie. It had a small but prosperous general store, a blacksmith and repair shop, a saddlery and harness shop, and one low building that housed the offices of Foster Bainbridge, attorney at law, and Harry Payne, M.D. Frank McNeil had few friends here. His line fence lay only a mile and a half to the north, a barrier to settlement that would have meant more business.

Scobie also had that most necessary of all frontier establishments, a well-run, a discreetly run, brothel. Ruby Potter's place was not really in the town, and her girls were never seen there. The merchants were unanimously her friends, since she attracted business that otherwise would have gone elsewhere.

Few people knew that Frank McNeil had known Ruby Potter thirty years ago and had bought the house in Scobie for her because it would keep his men healthy and at home. As a business proposition it paid off slowly but steadily. She got all the profits, but his men did not have to go into Merced for a high old time. There was no licensed saloon in Scobie, but Ruby sold whiskey and did not permit drunkenness or rowdy behavior.

Ruby had a few investments that Foster Bainbridge watched over for her. He had an appointment with her for this afternoon; so as soon as his brief conference with

Uncle Frank was over, Bainbridge excused himself, too. It was not a buggy he drove, but a single, aging horse pulling a rubber-tired racing sulky. He could go almost anywhere a rider could go and in a great deal more comfort.

He headed eastward, down the slope from the house. A mile from the house the well-rutted road curved around a rocky hillock where, a few years ago, Frank McNeil had had a road blasted through. On the left was a high heap of rock rubble; on the right, a sheer rock wall. Beyond the hillock was a somewhat higher hill covered by live oaks. From here it was a straight run to Scobie.

Bainbridge did not punish a horse, even though he knew he would be late for his appointment. He was rounding the rocky curve when he heard the shriek of a heavy bullet and the thud of it striking something.

He was a man of quick reactions. Just as his horse collapsed between the shafts, the lawyer leaped off the back end of the sulky, snatching the locked valise in which he carried his legal papers in his left hand and pulling a .45 that he wore on his belly under his coat with his right hand. The horse was down. He was still struggling feebly, but he had been hit in the heart or close to it and was as good as dead already.

Bainbridge thought he saw a man up among the live oaks on the next hill. It was too far a shot for a .45, but he put the valise down and gripped the gun in both hands and fired one anyway. He had the satisfaction of seeing the man sprint for cover over the hilltop, and then he heard the hoofbeats of a hard-ridden horse.

So far he had acted on instinct. Now he had time to think, and his chest began to tighten as he realized the plight he was in. Had the sniper wanted to kill him, it would have been an easy shot. What he wanted was the valise with the papers in it, and here Bainbridge was afoot on the trail with only five shots left in his gun with which to defend himself.

A moment later he heard hoofbeats of a cantering horse —no, it sounded like two horses—from the southwest, far from the house. He pitched the valise as high up in the rock pile as he could and saw it drop out of sight. The gun in his hand, he examined his sulky. It and the harness were undamaged, but his horse, a companion for more than ten years, was dead.

The thing to do was get out of here into the open prairie where he had a chance to see anyone approaching him. Still holding the .45, he began walking toward Scobie. The hoofbeats of the two horses came closer and closer.

Suddenly out of the brush came Pete Viscaino and another, younger, bigger, darker man. Bainbridge wiped the sweat from his eyes and holstered the gun. Whoever had shot at him, it wouldn't have been Pete.

"What the hell you doing here afoot, Foster?" Pete asked.

"This sun will kill you," said the other man, and Bainbridge now recognized him as Pete's eldest son, Marco.

"My horse was shot back there in the rock turn," Bainbridge said. "It was a deliberate ambush. I got a glimpse of the man but not enough to recognize him."

"Take my horse and ride up to the house and let them give you a new one."

"No. That's where the gunman came from. I don't want to give him a second chance, and I've got to get to Scobie."

Marco took his hat off and scratched his mop of brown curls. "Neither one of these damn brutes will carry double, Mr. Bainbridge. Let's see, how are we going to do this?"

Marco was riding a big, dark gelding. "Will your horse work in harness, do you think?" Bainbridge asked.

"Well, he can. He don't like it very well, but he has.
You driving a buggy?"

"A double-seated sulky. My rig isn't damaged. If we
could put your horse in the shafts and you could take me
to Scobie, I'd make it well worth your while."

"You talk like an idiot. Let's see what we're up against."

The Viscainos got the harness off the dead horse and the
saddle off Marco's. The horse did not like the shafts, but
Marco took no nonsense. It was a tight squeeze for the two
of them in the seat, neither being a small man, but they
made it.

Bainbridge said nothing about his valise in the rock pile.
That was the safest place for it for the time being. Pete
agreed to wait an hour before going to the house to report
the dead horse.

"Don't say a damn word about me being here," Marco
said. "I don't want to talk to that old son of a bitch of a
Frank about it or anything else."

"I'll let them figger I just came across the horse after
you'd left, but I won't lie outright," Pete said.

Once Marco's powerful horse reconciled himself to the
ignoble harness and shafts, he broke into an easy canter
that ate up the miles. Marco said he had come back for a
brief visit with his mother, as he often did, without letting
the McNeils know about it. They chatted as the sulky
drew them swiftly to Scobie.

"That little girl—let's see, Eloísa—her mother nurses the
old bastard—how is she?" Marco asked.

"I didn't see her today, but she has become one of the
loveliest women I've ever known."

"I used to be sweet on her when we was kids. I wish I
could see her, too, before I go back to Stockton."

"I'm afraid you're out of luck there, Marco. She and
young Terence McNeil seem to have a love affair going."

Marco cursed. "Sure, and I know what kind. He'll set her up in a *casita* and raise a bunch of kids by her to prove what a *macho* bastard he is, but he'll marry some Anglo woman with money and social standing. The way old Frank did her grandmother."

"I'm afraid I don't understand that."

"Hell, Eloísa's Frank's granddaughter. His wives both died without giving him a kid, and he took up with a Méxican housemaid. She had a son by him—let's see, Javier was his name, Javier Sánchez. Javier married old María González, only she was young María then. An American didn't marry a Méxican in those days unless forty or fifty thousand acres of land went with her."

"Let's get this straight. María is Frank's daughter-in-law in an illegitimate way, and Eloísa is the daughter of María and Frank's son."

"Didn't you know that?"

"No." Bainbridge knew that Frank had made provision for María and Eloísa in his will but not why, and he could not ethically reveal even that much.

"Ernest used to have a little money, too," Marco said. "He had a mercantile business in Oakland. He was too tight to get married, but he took up with a Méxican woman, and she had three kids for him. She was smart enough to see a lawyer when Ernest retired, and that's where his money went. That's why he had to come and live on Frank's charity."

"Where are they now?"

"God knows. The mother's probably dead. The kids would be middle-aged and scattered to hell and gone. That was thirty or forty years ago, anyway, that he closed out his business in Oakland."

It would not do to show too much interest in front of Marco, but Bainbridge knew where he might get information. There was little that Ruby Potter did not know about people, if she chose to talk. She rarely did.

He arrived in Scobie earlier than he would have behind his own tired old horse. Marco refused payment. He ran the sulky into the shed, hung up the harness, saddled his horse, and rode off. A bad man to have for an enemy, the lawyer decided, but the Viscainos were stout friends and generous people.

He did not take time to eat before heading for Ruby Potter's place. She had just installed a beer tap and ice chest, and over cooling steins of dark beer they talked a long time.

"I know you won't use any of this to get me into trouble," Ruby said. "I've got no use for that old bastard of a Frank, but I've got to get along with him. He gets more overbearing every day of his life, and it looks like he's going to live forever."

"He's a mighty healthy old man from a very long-lived family."

"Does he know about the tent show next Friday night? We're going to have one here in the plaza. I know some of the artists in it, and they're good. The least he could do is bring his outfit here and let them make a little money."

"Give me the names of the artists, and I'll send a man out with a note tomorrow."

"Well, Professor Means is head of it. He's a hypnotist and ventriloquist. His wife, I forget her name, is a whistler and the best I ever heard. Starts with birdcalls and then does popular melodies. There's a pair of soft-shoe sand dancers, a banjo trio, a couple of comedians—one of them is one of the banjoists—and the professor has worked them up into a fine chorus for the grand finale. Frank used to love a good show."

Bainbridge was writing busily. And early in the morning

a boy from the livery stable was on his way to the Dot M Dot with a note about the tent show. By now they would have discovered the dead horse and would wonder how he had got to Scobie. Let them! Ruby was not going to talk now, anyway.

Baron Godfrey had taken the Winchester Model 73 from the pegs on which it hung behind the kitchen door. There were guns all over the place, and this was the least likely to be missed. He managed to conceal it all the way back to the ranch. He cleaned it and oiled it deftly, quickly, but then had no opportunity to slip it back into the busy kitchen. He hid it in a wagon shed nearby and caught up with the fence crew before they reached their working site.

He did not offer to explain where he had been, and so long as he put in his day's work, Terence did not care. They finished the fence in midafternoon and started home.

Old Frank heard them coming and had María move his rocking chair out on the *pórtico*. He stood up and waved peremptorily to Terence again and again. Terence, with his mind on Eloísa, ignored him at first, but obviously the old man meant business. He sent the crew to put the teams and tools away and turned his horse up to where he could dismount at the foot of the three steps to the *pórtico*.

"Foster Bainbridge's horse was ambushed, shot through the ribs, down there at the rock pile," the old man said. "No sign Foster was hurt, and the harness and sulky are gone. Jesus Christ, not a mile from the house, and he didn't even come back here to tell us!"

"Maybe he figured somebody from here did it," said Terence.

The old man told a clear story; his mind had never been

sharper. Of course somebody from here had shot the horse! Not necessarily one of his own men, but the direction of the bullet was from here. He had sent Miguel, the most capable of his Méxican hands, down to read the sign as soon as he got word of a dead horse in the road.

"A pair of riders came along, prob'ly right after it happened. One horse shod on all four feet, one the front feet only, and he was a big one. The one shod all around headed toward Pete Viscaino's place, but he lost his sign in the grass.

"Looked like they hooked the other horse to Foster's sulky and drove him home thataway. It was a big horse, one thing. By God, Terence, if Pete Viscaino had a hand in this—"

"Oh, come on, Uncle Frank! Pete wouldn't shoot from ambush. You haven't got a more loyal man here than Pete."

Terence was some time calming Frank down. The old man was remembering other, more violent days, when things like assassinations and ambushes were not very newsworthy.

"Well," he said, when he was calmer, "if they didn't get Foster, they didn't get his portmanteau. You ride into Scobie tomorrow and see him. Get the whole story. And we owe him a horse, a good, fast harness horse. And a man to break him to the sulky. Take care of it for me, Terence, will you? Lord, lord, boy—I don't know what I'd do without you."

Toward evening, Baron Godfrey got the Winchester out of the wagon shed and strolled toward the back door of the house with it, carrying it vertically to hide as much of it as possible with his leg. He watched his chance, slipped into the kitchen, and hung the gun on its pegs. He was taking a drink of coffee from the pot on the stove when María came in.

She did not speak to him. He thanked her for the coffee, told her he had a headache, and went out. He sat down on a circular bench around a pepper tree and rolled and lighted a cigarette.

When the supper bell rang, he saw Ernest get with difficulty out of his hammock, brace himself on his cane, and head around the house toward the front door. Ernest spent his summer afternoons in the shade of a lath house in which some long-gone gardener had started seedings. Baron hurried to catch up with him where they would be out of sight, around the corner of the house.

"I told you you were crazy as hell," he greeted Ernest.

"In what way?" said Ernest.

"For shooting the horse instead of him. I had to get the rifle back before I could look for the papers. Fur as I know, they're still down there. I should have drilled the son of a bitch through the head."

Ernest shuddered delicately. "I can't condone even the thought of cold-blooded murder. What happened to Bainbridge?"

"I think somebody came along and hitched his horse to his sulky and took him home. Jesus Christ, did you expect me to stand around there and gawk? Frank sent Miguel down there. I don't know what they found out or if they got the valise. Maybe you can get it out of Frank at supper."

Ernest shook his head petulantly. "You have failed me miserably, and it will cost you more than it does me. Any new will—we have to assume this, we *have* to—will cut my inheritance to a mere pittance. What can there be in that for you?"

"How do you know there's a new will?"

"María and another Méxican witnessed it last week. I am not altogether a fool. If I could not keep track of my end of things any better than you, we would all starve. You've *got* to get hold of that new will and bring it to me so it can be destroyed."

"If it's destroyed, the old one still stands up?"

"Very likely. Help me to the house. Your news has shaken me. I feel terribly weak. But you mustn't try to eat at the family table tonight. There will be talk, and you are too transparent. I have lost a great deal of confidence in you, Baron."

But there was no talk at the dinner table other than the oddity of Bainbridge's horse being shot and his own disappearance. Terence had persuaded Frank to handle it that way. "It's still their move," he said. "Play it close to your chest, like aces back to back in a game of draw."

No one missed Baron Godfrey. No one noticed that Ernest drank a good deal of rum and ate very little food. Terence excused himself early.

"You know where he's going, don't you?" Julia demanded of Frank.

"No, and I don't care. His time's his own after his work is done."

She said spitefully, "He's conducting a shameless affair with that girl Eloísa, María's daughter, and María is conniving in it."

"The hell he is!"

"The hell he isn't!" Julia almost screamed at him. "Everyone in the Méxican quarters knows about it, but you know how they are."

"No," he said, "I don't. How are they?"

He grinned his ugly, mocking grin at her. She retreated into a dignified silence. Had she known that Eloísa was

Frank's illegitimate granddaughter, she might have made capital of it. But in ninety-four years, a man learned to keep shut-mouth about a few things around his female family folk, and Frank merely chuckled to himself as he thought how things had come full circle. He could barely remember what Eloísa's grandmother had looked like, only that she had been meek, adoring, compliant, and a hell of a lot smarter than she looked.

Many a time he had wished he had married her, but their son, Javier, had been pretty worthless. There was a lot to be said for old, established customs. Keep what's good, and dispose of what's not so good.

He had a hard time remembering Eloísa's grandmother's name. Josefina, that was it. It was Josefina who had spoiled Javier, their son. *Una tigra*, that woman. Well, everything worked out for the best if you lived long enough.

CHAPTER 4

Eloísa came to the house to help with the supper dishes. The zinc-lined redwood sink was at a western window, the hottest place possible. She was deft and skillful at whatever she did. The other women brought the dirty dishes and piled them on the table on her left after scraping them into the garbage pails for the hogs. Eloísa rapidly filled the sink compartment to the right. Terence came into the kitchen just in time to see her start to pick up the heavy teakettle of boiling water from the stove.

The other women scattered like quail when he said, "Here, let me." Everything on this place was on a big scale, and the three-gallon spouted kettles in which they boiled water were full.

"Careful," Eloísa said softly. "Don't scald yourself, just the dishes."

Few Méxican men would be caught helping a woman with her kitchen work. Terence knew that it was a source of pride to Eloísa that he had no such inhibitions where she was concerned. He poured the water over the clean, soapy dishes, filled the teakettle, and set it back on the stove. Eloísa took a big huck towel and began to wipe the scalded ones.

The glisten of perspiration made her face glow, made her skin look transparent, so that a light dusting of freckles leaped out under her eyes, and on her cheeks. She had freckles on her body, too. Today her breasts were primly banded and she wore a loose, long skirt of some ugly checked combination of garish colors. He leaned against the table and watched how gracefully she moved as she wiped the dishes.

They had the kitchen to themselves for a long time. When she stopped clattering dishes into stacks as she dried them and reached for the pots and pans, he took a step closer to her. She turned to face him, wiping her hands on her apron.

"You could kiss me now if you do it quickly," she said.

He tried to take her in his arms, but she did not mean to get caught in a shameless posture by the other women. She held his upper arms and put her face up, and he kissed her open mouth again and again. Their tongues touched, and he clutched at her buttocks. Again she evaded him, but he saw that he had brought color to her cheeks.

"Tonight?" he asked. She shook her head, and he went on, "Why not? It doesn't have to be in your house. I'll hook up a team to a buggy and we'll go somewhere."

Again she shook her head. "Women's reasons."

"How's that?"

"I just started my period. You ought to be glad."

"I'm not sure I am."

"Terence, what would you do if you got me with child?"

"Why, we'd get married. What did you think?"

"I wonder if you really would. Your uncle would tell you it is not necessary with a Méxican girl. He would give us a little house where you could spend as much or as little time as you liked, and I would always be there."

He watched his chance and whacked her soundly across her firm little bottom. "Uncle Frank doesn't make my decisions for me, sweetheart."

"Terence, why have you never married?"

"I've never found the woman I want to marry."

"Do you think you have now?"

He had to be honest with her. "Honest to God, I don't know. I can't see myself staying here on the Dot M Dot much longer. I wonder how happy you'd be living somewhere else. I'd have to get a job. I've got a little money but not enough to keep a family."

"Maybe it's a good thing. You have to think it out carefully, and what you decide will be right."

"Do you have to think it out, too?"

She did not answer but turned to her work at the sink. He understood that he had been dismissed, and he did not mind. What a wise little thing she was, to think so coolly when she loved him so hotly! He was fairly sure that she and her mother had discussed this very thing many times, and he did not mind. María was wise and worldly, and she was his friend.

He had made it a habit to patrol the place on horseback and on foot every evening. You always found gates open that should not be open, things left out that should have been put away, livestock whose water troughs had run dry. Uncle Frank paid thirty a month, good money for a steady and fairly easy job. But a cowboy was not paid to take certain responsibilities, and Frank's did not.

When he finished his rounds he picked up a lamp in the kitchen and went up to his room. He lighted another lamp there and began the difficult job of writing to his mother. She was only in her forties and still beautiful, and all she was ever interested in was men. Every letter he got from her—and they were not numerous—was about some new lover who was different from all the other men in the world.

The last letter had been written a month and a half ago from New York, and the man was a wealthy jeweler, a widower of sixty who was willing to put one hundred and

twenty thousand dollars in trust for her, the income to
accrue during his lifetime and be paid, along with portions
of the principle, to her after his death. Meanwhile he
would give her an allowance of six hundred dollars a month
for personal spending money. His name was E. David
Franzenheimer, and what seemed to disturb his mother
most was being known as Mrs. Franzenheimer.

The best way to handle it was to ignore Mr. Franzenheimer altogether, because before his letter could get to
her, chances were she would have another candidate. She
did not seem to realize that she would be getting old soon,
she was already losing the bloom of beauty, and could not
play the coquette forever. He wrote her the kind of letter
an affectionate father would write a nitwit daughter of
whom he was very fond, saying, among other things:

> Above all, it is time for you to remarry. Who the
> man is, I leave to your judgment. I know you will
> choose wisely, but I cannot be at peace with the conti-
> nent between us and you without a man to watch over
> you. Try to begin to think of it in terms of friendship,
> companionship, and the security you deserve. I am
> certain that my father would give the same advice,
> straight from his heart. Look at it this way—a beauti-
> ful woman is like an expensive jewel that requires a
> guard.

He did not mention Uncle Frank. Frank had met his
sister-in-law, Elena, only once and had not much respect
for her. But then Frank did not like any Italian.

Terence's room was larger than he needed and had once
been Ernest's. Frank had had Ernest moved to one just as
comfortable, but it had no connecting door with his own.
The old man insisted that the door between his bedroom
and Terence's be left open all night. Terence had assumed

that the old man was sound asleep, but now he heard him speak.

"Terence, what you doing with two lamps burning in there? Hard as you work, you need your sleep."

"Just finishing a letter to Mother. I'll have them out in a minute."

He undressed, blew out both lamps, and was just getting into bed when old Frank called again.

"I woked up and can't get back to sleep. Come in and talk to me a minute."

Resignedly Terence got up in his underwear and went into his uncle's room. Frank told him to light a candle; no sense burning a lamp, as expensive as coal oil was. Terence lighted the candle on the bedside table and sat down in the little armless rocking chair that had belonged to Uncle Frank's first wife seventy years ago.

Frank lay on his back, propped up on several goose-down pillows, with a *sarape*, a cotton blanket of Méxican weave, over him. He put his hands behind his head and made himself comfortable.

"Terence," he said, "what do you make of this goddamned business today, killing Foster's horse."

"Well, I don't think it was an accident."

"Hell, only a fool would think that! What do you think it was?"

"I think somebody thought Mr. Bainbridge would panic and come running back to the house, leaving his heavy valise in the wreckage. That's what they wanted, the papers he was carrying. To me that's as plain as the nose on your face."

"My idea exactly. Where was Baron Godfrey while this was going on?"

Terence frowned. "He was with my crew, but I'm not

sure when he joined us. We're not exactly chums, and he doesn't seek my companionship."

"He'd be a bad one with that forty-five. You still don't go armed, do you?"

"No. You might as well carry a peashooter as a thirty-eight, and a forty-five is too big for my hand."

"When did you learn that?"

"In military academy."

"You've growed since then. Your hand has *got* to be big enough to handle one now. I'm going to give you my own. I've never fired it. Smokeless powder came out about the time I took to my bed, when I had the lung fever. Let's see, when was that? Early seventies? My memory ain't even a memory now. Jesus, that stuff kicked like a mule! It was too much for me but you can handle it. The gun's in that drawer there. Get it out."

Terence took out the heavy .45 and examined it. It was in perfect condition and was an ornate weapon with real ivory grips in which the old man's cattle brand, the Dot M Dot, had been engraved by an expert. He hefted it in his hand.

"Feels as heavy as a three-pounder cannon to me, Uncle Frank."

"Because you haven't developed the muscles for it. Tomorrow María will give you a box of ca'tridges for it, and I'll order some more. I want you to take that and wear it— María will give you a holster to suit you—and I want you to shoot up a box of a hundred ca'tridges a day until you're master of that weapon."

"All right, and thank you." It was easier to give in than argue, and the chance to learn to handle so fine a gun was not to be passed up.

"Way to learn to shoot fast and straight is to draw on everything. Tin cans is good. Learn to keep hitting them and rolling them ahead of you until you're out of shots. Then see how many hits you made."

"I'll try that."

"Chickens is good, too. But ask María which ones you can shoot. You kill one of her laying hens, and she'll feed you garbage for a week."

"Uncle Frank, do you suspect that Baron Godfrey had something to do with killing that horse?"

"I'd bet on it. I used to keep track of the guns here. Knowed where every damn one of 'em was. In the old days the Méxican bandits could ride down out of the hills and raid the bejesus out of you and be gone before you could get to a gun cabinet. So I kept Winchesters and Henrys everywhere. Nobody keeps track of them anymore."

"I'll kind of take an inventory of them and see that they're kept where they're supposed to be kept. But if Baron is capable of something like that, why not just get rid of him? He's not much of a worker."

Frank cackled. "No, I like to see him around ass-kissing Ernest. They all think I drawed a new will and that's what Foster had in the valise. Hell of a lot of good it would do them to get them papers."

"It's a risky business at best, Uncle Frank."

"Not if you can outshoot Baron. I hear you been going down there to bed down with María's daughter a lot lately. Mighty fine girl, ain't she?"

The abrupt change of topic caught Terence by surprise. "Too fine a girl to be the subject of gossip around here. Where did you hear it?"

"From her mother. And the Méxicans all know it. You could have your pick of the Méxican girls, but you chose the right one."

"What would you say if I married her?"

"Better think that over. Better let me think it over, too.

You don't have to marry her. The Méxicans like me and trust me, and they like you and trust you. I been their *patrón* all my life. Now they think you're going to be their *patrón*. Eloísa would keep you happy whether you married her or not."

"I don't like that way of doing things."

Again his uncle switched topics with lightning speed. "Your mother ever tell you about Fanny Bannister?"

"No. I've never heard the name."

"About the only thing Elena and me ever agreed on. Fanny's a widow, lives in San Francisco, coming here to visit us any day. Your ma wants you to marry her, and she'd make you a good wife, and she wouldn't interfere if you kept a *casita*."

"No thanks, Uncle Frank."

The old man ignored him. "She come from dirt-poor folks, and she married a man that would've made a fortune if he'd lived. Poor devil, he had so much to live for."

"What did he do for a living?"

"Ran a tannery. I'd think your mother would've told you about them. Louis Bannister was your father's godson. Him and Fanny was married when she was only sixteen, and he was stabbed in a holdup when she was twenty-two. I send her a little check every now and then."

Terence said nothing. The old man stretched restlessly. "Play me some music," he said. "That's what I need when I'm nervous like this. Nothing calms me down like that fiddle of yours."

There was no way out. Terence went to his room and and got the violin out and tuned it by ear. Uncle Frank, oddly enough, did not like the stomp music of the frontier. He liked Bach and Mozart, the light, spirited, tinkling tunes you kept hearing long after the instrument was silent. Terence had brought no sheet music with him, and he could not remember all he wished he could, but he could improvise, and the old man didn't know the difference anyway.

He could hear Julia angrily banging things in her bedroom, and he supposed Frank could hear her, too, but what Julia thought was the least of Frank's worries. Terence played for perhaps thirty minutes, until he thought the old man was alseep.

"Funny the dogs didn't hear it," came his sleepy voice.

"Hear what?"

"When that horse of Foster's was shot."

"It's a long way away. Wind was probably in the east. I've never heard these dogs make any fuss about a gunshot, anyway."

"I had the fellers drag the horse off to where the coyotes can clean him to bones before he makes a stink there. They said it was a forty-four, at least. Have you ever shot a Winchester rifle of that bore?"

"Many times."

"They kick like hell. Whoever dropped that horse in one shot knowed what he was doing with a gun." Uncle Frank laboriously raised himself on his elbow. "Fetch me a drink of that good rum, and then I think I could sleep, and tomorrow you start checking out the guns on this place. I know there's at least five or six Winchesters, seventies or seventy-threes, all forty-four caliber. Don't say anything to anybody; just kind of nose around and see what you turn up."

Terence brought the old man a triple shot of rum and held him up while he sipped it. Dr. Payne might not like such a big dose, but this, he had said, was good medicine for an old man who couldn't get to sleep. Frank drank only about half of it before he began to nod. Terence lowered him to the bed and then carried the half-filled glass into his own room.

On impulse he slipped on his pants and started barefoot down the stairs. As he passed Julia's door, he heard her say, "I'll thank God on my knees the day that fellow goes home. Keeping a body awake all night with that screeching fiddle at my age!"

She must have been talking to Ernest. Terence heard what sounded like Ernest's voice replying, but he could not make out the words.

He knew that a Winchester Model 73, a .44 caliber, hung on pegs behind the kitchen door. He groped his way through the kitchen, and even before he laid hands on the weapon, he knew he had found the gun that had killed the lawyer's horse. Someone had recently swabbed the barrel with solvent to remove lead traces from the lands and then with light oil to rust-proof it against the solvent. The gun reeked of both odors.

Who had easy access to this gun? Anyone who watched his chance and waited until the kitchen women were out. He replaced the rifle on its pegs and went back to bed.

But not to sleep. Now his mother and Uncle Frank had picked out a wife for him, a widow older than himself, one who presumably would let him keep Eloísa in a little love nest in the México *barrio*. He was drawing exactly one hundred and fifty dollars a month, good pay, but he did two men's work and had the responsibility for the whole ranch.

Three blooded stallions. Eighty acres of cultivated pasture where Frank raised blooded bulls. Probably four thousand head of good beef cattle on the range. Nearly five hundred horses, most of which should have gone to market long ago and which he was expected to get ready for the market as early as possible.

And his biggest responsibility of all was a man ninety-four years of age who had never taken a word of advice in his life, who was surrounded by treachery in his own family. An old fool who was determined to live to be one hundred years old in this environment and who used his riches to tantalize those almost as old who expected to inherit. A man who dribbled out monthly payments as though giving children their allowances: to Ernest and Julia, and God knows how much they received, and now, he knew, to this Fanny Bannister.

Time I had a little talk with Foster Bainbridge. Get a horse broken to the sulky, he thought, and safe to turn over to him. And then get the hell out of here as fast as I can.

CHAPTER 5

Foster Bainbridge's lengthy note about the tent show arrived as the family was sitting down to breakfast in the big dining room. Terence could not help noticing the looks of apprehension on the faces of Ernest and Julia as it was brought in by a servant. The off-white, heavy envelope and the heavy black handwriting were familiar to all of them by now.

"Bring that boy in here, and set a place for him," Uncle Frank said. "If he's come from Foster this morning, he needs feeding." He blinked helplessly at the envelope, than handed it to Terence. "Here, read this to me. My eyes ain't what they used to be."

He was completely confident that the envelope would not contain a confidential message, which might or might not mean something. Terence slit the envelope with his pocketknife and read the letter aloud. Julia hastened to get in the first comment.

"What does he take us for, ignorant hicks?" she snapped. "Why, I've heard the de Reszkes in Vienna; I've seen the—what was the name of those wonderful French pantomimists?"

Frank paid no attention to her. "Hey, we'll have a fiesta. Knock off early and let the whole gang go in. Get the carriage out and dust it off and put on two good teams. Nothin' I love better than a good music hall show."

"This is *not* a music hall show," Julia said. "It is a fraud, a medicine show, a tasteless display." She looked at Ernest. "Ernest, you're surely not going. You couldn't possibly be interested in this."

Ernest declined to meet her eyes. "I don't know, Julia. Any excuse for an outing. You'll go, won't you? You won't want to stay around here alone."

"Surely the Méxicans won't go!"

"Hell they won't!" Frank cackled. "They love a show better'n anybody. Terence, you tell the boys, and then see how much work you can get out of them. Let's see, this is Wednesday. If we knock off Friday at noon—hell, you ought to get three days' work out of them before then. And read it to María. She'll tell the Méxicans."

Julia surrendered in silence. Terence went out to break the news to the crew, whose members were just getting their horses out. The whoop that went up showed how they felt about it. Even Baron Godfrey grinned.

He thought of going to tell Eloísa about it himself, but it was too conspicuous. Besides, he would not be able to spend much time with her in Scobie at the show. The crew never required more supervision than when they were on a holiday. Scobie had a resident deputy sheriff, an able man by the name of Bill Marquant, but he concerned himself mostly with serving summonses and notices of tax delinquencies. He would be worse than useless if rowdyism got out of hand.

And even as he was rereading Bainbridge's letter to the crew for the third time, two hard-running teams on a top buggy came, soaked with sweat, up the same road down that Bainbridge had driven the other day to his horse's death. The driver hauled them in with a flourish in front of the house. María came out and called for someone to help a woman descend from the buggy and bring in her bags.

Terence knew who it was without being told. Fanny

Bannister! She was rather short and attractively buxom, and her fair hair glinted in the sun. He knew that Frank would soon be sending for him.

One of the pumps had stopped working. He picked two men to help him rig a block and tackle in the top of the windmill to pull the column of water-filled pipe so he could repair the cylinder at the bottom. They had half the column piled and stacked upright inside the windmill tower and he was thoroughly soaked and covered with mud when one of the kitchen women came to tell him that the señor wanted him at the house immediately.

He left instructions with the men for pulling the rest of the column, mounted the only saddle horse they had brought, and rode down to the house. He knew he was expected to make himself presentable before coming in to meet Mrs. Bannister, and he could have slipped upstairs and changed. But he deliberately went through the house to the living room in the clothing in which he had been working on the well.

He acknowledged the woman's presence with a bow. She was startlingly beautiful; it would be easy to underestimate her age under the spell of that exquisite blonde loveliness. His uncle was in his big rocking chair beside the cold fireplace, next to the four posts that supported his big iron safe upstairs.

"You wanted to see me?"

"Yes," Uncle Frank said angrily, "I do, and I wanted you to clean up and be fit to meet a lady. Go up and change and come back down."

Mrs. Bannister arose from her chair and held out her hand with a smile. "That won't be necessary, Mr. McNeil. I know that working men get dirty. I'm Fanny Bannister, and I know your mother, and my late husband used to be your father's companion of many a fishing trip."

"How do you do. It is such a pleasure to know you," he said, taking the firm and friendly clasp of her hand.

The man, he thought, did not live who would not respond to this beauty and magnetic sensuality. She knew how to dress as few western women did, and she had the lush figure for it. She was wearing a linen suit today that showed a minimum of travel stain and had just laid aside a straw hat with a blue veil and a cluster of blue flowers on it. Her tiny feet were shod in fawn-colored shoes laced with blue.

Her eyes were blue, too deep and smoky blue. Her face was round, merry-looking; her mouth large, mobile, and red-lipped—and kissable. Here was a woman with a passionate disposition and an easily triggered temper, a woman used to having her own way in most things.

Before sitting down, she started to remove the jacket of the suit. He moved to help her. Under it she wore a prim white shirtwaist against which her sumptuous breasts pressed hard. They were breasts meant to be fondled and kissed, and he knew it and knew that she knew he knew it.

"Fanny hired a rig and came a-hellin' up from Merced," Frank said. "She's goin' to spend a few weeks here and go to the tent show with us Friday. She's heard this whistling woman."

"Orlena Means. She and her husband are both exquisite artistes, and they wouldn't have anyone in their company who is not the best."

As far as Uncle Frank was concerned, it was settled. Mrs. Bannister had been on the road since last evening. She wanted a bath and a nap. "You get whatever you're doing finished," Frank said to Terence, "and then you hook up the buckskins to the light buggy and take her for a ride around the place."

"And you must play your violin for me soon, too," Mrs. Bannister said. "They say you're so good!"

"That's my mother talking. I'm not a performer. Usually you'll find me in the audience somewhere."

He made his excuses and was not a little disturbed to find that the woman had made a strong impression on him. He felt uneasy, as though he was being led into something attractive but not for him, and he did not know what to do about it.

He returned to the well. When he came in at noon, the cylinder had been repaired and they had started to lower the column into the drilled hole, screwing on the pipe a section at a time as they lowered it. Frank asked him about it and nodded in a pleased fashion.

"Fine! They can finish up with the well. You get changed and take Fanny for a ride. She'll be down for dinner—she calls it luncheon—in about an hour. You've got time for a bath and some clean clothes before you come to eat, and then you take her for a spin around the ranch."

He went up to his room. Eloísa had set the galvanized tub in the center of it and had half filled it with warmish water. From the first it had annoyed him that her mother had been expected to attend him as he bathed, but that was the custom here, and he had got used to it. Now, to find Eloísa at the same task was doubly embarrassing, especially since he was getting ready to take another woman for a ride.

He put his hands on her shoulders. "Eloísa, who told you to do this? I can't have you being my servant."

"Mamá told me to do it," she said demurely. "What is wrong with it?" She knelt before him. "Here, let me take your boots and get out your new ones."

"Nothing doing. You beat it. I'll bathe and change myself."

She began unbuttoning his shirt. "No, Mamá will be very angry at both of us. *Por favor*, Terence, let us hurry, or she'll be up here."

Feeling like a fool, he undressed and stepped into the tub. She knelt and handed him the dripping washcloths and then the towel. On her face was the wholly fictitious expression of subservience against which he had no defense. You see, she was saying, if there is to be another woman here, Mamá means that you do not forget me, and so do I. . . . When he was shaved, dry, and still naked, he attempted to put his arms around her. She eluded him deftly.

"Oh no! One woman at a time," she said. "Let me help you dress."

"Goddamn it," was all he could say.

He put on a white shirt and the blue trousers to a suit that he had not worn since his arrival here. He spent a little time selecting a tie and then changed his mind and went down to the dining room without either coat or tie. As he left, Eloísa was dipping up the water from his tub to throw out the upstairs window on a flower bed below. She still wore that same demure smile.

"Hell of a way to come to the table," Frank said. He and Fanny were already seated at one end of the big table. Ernest and Julia were not present.

He sat down across from the woman, at his uncle's right. "I'm sorry, Mrs. Bannister, but I've fallen into some pretty informal habits here. So has Uncle Frank. He hasn't had a necktie on since I've been here."

"My name is Fanny," she said, "and I'm going to call you Terence. I'm glad you wore no tie. It would spoil the atmosphere completely."

María served them personally. First she brought them a salad made of crisp leaf lettuce with a spicy Méxican dressing; and then, enchiladas. Fanny, it seemed, loved Méxican cooking, especially enchiladas.

María's manner was cold, even to Frank. When she put the coffeepot down on the pad and walked out without serving them, her message was clear: Let Mrs. Bannister pour! And if you're interested in this woman, Señor Terence, leave my Eloísa alone!

To his confusion, Terence found it hard to take his eyes off Fanny. She had changed from the shirtwaist to a cool, loose blouse that sagged one way or the other with every movement of her bust. The top button was not buttoned, and when she leaned forward, he could see the deep cleavage that was daintily powdered with scented powder. She leaned forward fairly often.

After lunch he got out the buckskins and hitched them to a light open buggy. They were not a young team, but they were old Frank's favorites, and they did not get much work. They were frisky enough to put on a show that Fanny enjoyed.

He headed eastward up the slope, letting the buckskins run the ginger out. They had slowed down to a more sedate pace about a mile from the house when Terence saw Pete Viscaino riding toward him, angling toward him from his own house and waving his hat. Terence pulled the team to a stop and waited for him.

Pete tipped his hat to Fanny. "Like to talk to you a minute in private, Terence, if the lady will excuse us," he said.

"Surely." He looked at Fanny. "Can you hold the team? They're through showing off."

"I've been dying to get my hands on the lines. I'm a good driver," she cried.

He handed them to her and jumped out of the buggy. She chirped to the team and handled them well as she drove them forty or fifty feet ahead.

Pete got down out of the saddle. "I told Marco I was going to tell you this," he said, "but he says you have to keep it to yourself because he couldn't prove nothing."

"Sure, what is it?"

"It was Baron Godfrey shot Bainbridge's horse."

"I half suspected it. How does your son know?"

"Saw him with the rifle and laid low. Baron tied in the clump of live oaks on the knoll just before you get to the rock curve and fired from the ground. Marco stayed hid, you can damn well believe!"

"Somebody wants to look at those papers pretty badly. He used the gun from the kitchen. It has been freshly swabbed and oiled. I made sure of that myself."

"Something else. I saw Baron and Ernest talking together just before suppertime. Ernest was giving him hell. Baron wouldn't do anything like that on his own. But he'd take orders."

"Oh come on, Pete, Ernest wouldn't conspire in a murder!"

"It wasn't a murder. All he meant was to shoot the horse and get the valise, but Foster began firing at him with a forty-five, and he had to get the hell out of there," Pete said.

"Point is, they're afraid old Frank is leaving his property to you. I've knowed them longer than you have, and Julia's just as bad as Ernest. They can't wait for the old boy to die."

"They're wasting a lot of energy. I'm not interested in Frank's money."

"Try to prove it to them. That's Marco's hunch—that if they can't destroy the will, they'll kill you."

He thanked Pete, who said, "There's damn little I owe Frank McNeil, but I draw the line at murder, and you've always been square with me. Just don't let on where you got the information."

Pete went on his way, and Terence got back into the buggy with Fanny and took the lines. He spent two hours taking her around the nearby Dot M Dot land. She saw fat cattle grazing on range that could have supported twice as many. She saw fine horses that should have gone to market long ago. She saw wealth that survived and grew despite the indecision and forgetfulness and slack hand of a man of ninety-four.

"Constructive avarice," she murmured.

"How's that?"

"Most big, important fortunes are built by men motivated by avarice. Not ownership for its own sake, but for what can be done with it. Surely you've known some millionaires."

"A few."

"How many have lacked the trait of avarice?"

"I've never thought of it, but I suppose not one."

"Stop here," she said. "Let's rest the team and get out of the buggy a moment."

They were on an open hillside from which the top of the house was barely visible. There were cattle not far away, including a couple of range bulls that could be dangerous, black Angus crossed with black Méxican longhorns bred for the bull ring. He cautioned her about them as he helped her out of the buggy.

She came out in his arms, yielding to lean her shapely, soft body against his. He could feel those intrusive breasts against his chest. He could smell her perfume and the clean, exciting perspiration of a lovely, heated body.

She did not let go of him. Her eyes met his levelly. Her big, soft lips parted, but although she was panting lightly, she remained in control of herself. "Terence," she whispered, "kiss me. I know you know how to kiss. Kiss me so I'll always remember it!"

He could not help himself when she put her hand on the back of his neck and brought his face toward her. Her hands dropped to press his body closer to her by pulling at his hips. He could not help the response he knew she felt.

She raised one hand to unbutton two of the buttons on her blouse. A little twist of her shoulders and both breasts fell free. She took his wrists to put his hands on them and said, "Oh God, that's what I want you to do. Harder, harder! Oh God, oh God!"

He did not know what would have happened had not the buckskins jumped, making the buggy lurch. A dozen cattle were trotting down the hill, led by two of those long-horned black bulls. He pulled himself free, cried, "Oh Jesus, Fanny—back into the buggy!" He put his hand under her bottom, swung her up, and dumped her on the seat.

One of the bulls and then the other broke into a run. Terence jumped in beside her, forcing her to make room. He snatched the whip out of the socket as one of the bulls put his head down and launched himself at the buggy.

He stood up and gave the bull a hard lash with all his strength across the face with it. The bull flinched. He stroked both horses sharply, and they broke into a smooth, fast gallop that the bulls could not hope to keep up with. Fanny, her blue eyes wide with puzzlement, looked behind her and screamed, "Oh my God, oh no!"

"Just hang onto me," he said.

He had to run the team only a few hundred yards before the bulls gave up. Fanny fell back against the seat and closed her eyes. Her blouse was still open, her bosom exposed.

"Oh Christ, I've never been so close to death before," she said.

"It was my fault for stopping."

"I wanted you to. I wanted to be kissed. I—I still do."

"Not now, and you'd better button up, Fanny. You're making a hell of an enchanting exhibition of yourself, in case you haven't noticed."

She narrowed her eyes as she adjusted her clothing. "I was blind to everything but you," she said, "but you had room for something else in your mind."

"You develop hair-trigger nerves on this job."

She studied him. "Your mother wants us to get married. You see, I'm being quite candid. She says it's the only way you'll ever get Frank McNeil's money—enough of it to make any difference."

"My mother's a born conspirator, and she doesn't know what she's talking about."

"Are you sorry we were interrupted?

He did not meet her eyes. "Nope."

"Why not?"

"Wrong time, wrong place, wrong reasons."

"And wrong woman. Frank told me about your Méxican girl. Are you so deeply in love with her?"

"I'm not sure, Fanny."

"She could cost you a million dollars. You and I could have an understanding that you could have her, too, after we inherited everything."

"It's not that important, and besides, Uncle Frank is a long way from dying."

"You've never been dirt poor, Terence. I have. I couldn't stand it again. That's why I would be willing for you to have the Méxican girl, too. It would work out."

"I doubt it, Fanny. I've seen too many of my mother's serialized romances. I'm not very sophisticated that way."

"That comes with age and maturity." She squeezed his arm, unoffended. "I like you very much, Terence, aside from the feeling of desire I have for you."

"I like you, too, Fanny, but I'm not a candidate for a husband."

"Thank you for saving my life, anyway. That's something I'll always remember. Now I'm beginning to get really frightened. My legs are shaky. Can—can those bulls get to the house?"

"No, I'll open this gate, and we'll go through it and close it behind us, and you're safe."

"Not from everything," she said, and he wondered if he might not be in the same position.

CHAPTER 6

Escaping the house early and taking two men to help him, Terence cut out one of the black bulls, ran him over to a pasture several miles away, and closed the gate on him and his new harem. It was not an easy job to separate him from the first bunch. He had to be roped and thrown, roped and thrown, several times before he got the idea that they meant business.

"Bulls is queer critters," said one of the cowboys. "They'll run at each other like locomotives to fight over a cow in heat and neglect the job to fight it out. But you try to separate them, and they're pals."

"Dogs is the same way," said the other man. "So are human beings when it comes to that. Two men hot on the same girl are going to fight it out some time or other, but until it comes to a showdown, they're pals. Look back there behind you."

The transplanted bull had already found a cow almost ready to breed and had begun his courtship of her. The first cowboy said, "I wish I had a job like that. Or like a studhorse. Get paid for it. So far, I've always been on the payin' end."

They came jogging back to the house late in the morning. Instantly Terence saw the red and green gourd dipper hanging on the windmill. He sent the two men to other duties, tied his horse in the shade, and carried the dipper to the back door of María's house. Eloísa opened it instantly at his knock. She was fully dressed, even to shoes, and she had just washed and dried her hair and let it hang in two big braids down her back.

She kissed him but she evaded his arms. "No, not today," she said. "Today we've got to talk."

She pointed to a chair. He sat down in it.

"About what?" he said.

"About Señora Bannister."

"What about her?"

"Mamá says Señor Frank brought her here to marry you."

"He thinks he did, and maybe she does, too, but I've got something to say about that."

She narrowed her lovely, dark eyes thoughtfully. "Even if it means losing all of Señor Frank's money?"

He shrugged. "I haven't got it now. I never have had it. I never planned on having it, and I've been perfectly happy."

"But you don't want to marry me."

He got up and moved restlessly around the small room. It was an ordeal not to put his hands on her while he talked, but to do so would be unfair. She did not mean to be distracted, and María, her mother, did not mean for her to be distracted, and yet she was as aflame with desire as he.

"I never said I didn't want to marry you," he said. "All I've ever said is that I doubt that I can support you. I've been trained for two things, the Army and to be a violinist, and I'm not very good at either. That's the trouble with having a little money, Eloísa, yet not enough to redesign your life. There is not one single job that appeals to me enough to make me want to make it a career."

"Not even running the Dot M Dot?"

He shook his head. "I'm not cut out for it."

"You do a good job. Mamá says Señor Frank is very

proud of you. You have the gift of decision, he says, and that's the most important thing if you're going to run a big thing like the Dot M Dot?"

"It would help if I enjoyed what I was doing, sweetheart."

She shook her head sadly. "Don't call me that. It breaks my heart. I'm not your sweetheart. What am I? You would forget me the day after tomorrow if you left here. No, no."

Her voice rose imperiously as he tried to interrupt. He knew that if he left the chair and took a step toward her, she would simply go into the other room, where her mother slept and where he was always ill at ease.

"I will tell you a few things you don't know, I think," she went on. "*La casita*, the little house, is part of the Méxican way of living. A boy and a girl fall in love, but they can't afford the priest's fees and the California fees, so they live together in *unión libre*, free union. Most marriages on this ranch are like that. No one thinks any less of it except the priests, and they put up with it because it means more babies for baptism in the Holy Church.

"But if the boy is ambitious and makes a lot of money, he does not marry the girl. At least I never heard of it happening. No, he gets another little house and another girl and makes sure he gets sons by having a family by her. It is very necessary for a Méxican man to prove he is a stallion that he is very male, do you understand me?"

"I know all about that. Eloísa darling, I've had you offered to me that way by Uncle Frank, and I told him to go to hell."

"If you married Señora Bannister."

"Yes. Even she consents to it—now. You don't know American women if you think she would put up with it very long. I know the kind of decision I face, my dear, and

I'm having no trouble at all making up my mind. I am not going to marry Fanny Bannister, and I am not going to set you up in a *casita*."

The tears came to her eyes. She said, "Then I will tell you something you do not know. My *mamacita* is a very wise woman. She has lived here all her life, and she has Señor Frank's *confianza*. So far she has never betrayed it except to me, but she wants me to tell you about it now. Terence, you and I are cousins."

"What!"

As though recounting a lesson she had memorized and repeated by rote many times, she told him about his Uncle Frank McNeil. In 1814, when he was twenty, Frank had married Lydia, a girl of sixteen. She died in 1820, leaving no children. Two years later he married Martha, an only daughter of a well-to-do merchant from Indiana. Shortly after her parents died and left her nearly forty thousand dollars. Martha, too, died without issue, in 1846.

Frank was then fifty years old, at the peak of his vigor, and he had just bought the property that was the home place and the nucleus of what was to become the Dot M Dot. Among the Méxicans living there was a descendant of the original grantee, Josefina Sánchez, twenty, pretty, nubile, and ambitious. She became his mistress, even at times sleeping in the big house. It was not so big then as it was now, but it was still where the mistress of the place lived.

She bore Frank a son in 1852 and named him Javier. When Javier was nineteen, in 1871, he married María González, another native of the place. By then Frank and Josefina had separated. When Javier wanted to go to Stockton to go into business, Frank gave him the money, and his mother went with him. He was killed in a waterfront brawl, and his doting mother did not long survive him.

It would have been ancient history, irrelevant to today, except that Javier's wife, María, refused to go to Stockton and live under the thumb of the shrewish mother-in-law, Josefina, who could not even get along with Uncle Frank, to whom she owed everything. María's daughter was born when María was fourteen, eighteen years ago. María named her Eloísa.

"So you see," Eloísa said, "Señor Frank is my grandfather. He has made my mother his *llavera*. Do you know what that means?"

"No."

"The keeper of the keys. It is more than a housekeeper. She has got rid of more than one manager. When you and I fell in love, it was a dream come true to her. Even first cousins marry in México, and we are not that closely related."

"Let's see," he said, "as nearly as I can figure it out, you and I are first half cousins once removed. You're the prettiest and nicest girl I have ever known, and I love you, and I have already told you why I am afraid to ask you to marry me. What would your mother say if I married you and took you away and got a job somewhere?"

"She would be desolated. She witnessed your Uncle Frank's new will a little while ago. She did not get to read it, but she heard Señor Frank and the *abogado*, the lawyer, talking about it many times. Almost all of his money and property goes to you. But he said just yesterday that if you did not marry Fanny Bannister, the hell with you, he would leave it to her."

"Let him. What's his fascination with her?"

"He is an old man. He would marry her himself if he could, but the next best thing is to make her rich. Mamá says if you do not marry her, he will see Señor Bainbridge and make still another will."

He wondered where María—and Eloísa herself—figured in all these wills and what provision had been made for poor Ernest and Julia. It was no wonder that María, after a lifetime of service to the old devil, would feel a proprietary interest in his estate. It was no wonder that Ernest and Julia, who had already outlived their normal life-spans, would be slightly cracked on the subject.

"In other words," Terence said, "your mother expects me to avoid marriage with Fanny without annoying Uncle Frank enough to make him change his will. And you and I may not be married unless I am his principal heir."

The troubled girl remained silent. Terence studied her carefully. He could see no resemblance to Frank McNeil at all in her unless it was the light dusting of freckles under her tawny skin. There were many Méxicans lighter in complexion than she. But her figure was taller than most Méxican girls', and she lacked entirely the thickness of torso of her mother.

One thing was sure, Frank McNeil was not the only hard-minded conspirator on the Dot M Dot. María González could match him queen for queen, pawn for pawn, except that he held physical possession of the most of the pieces. If she had Eloísa, Uncle Frank had Fanny.

He got up and crossed the room, put his hand on the back of her chair, and leaned over to kiss her. She avoided giving him her lips, and he kissed her forehead instead.

"I'm not exactly overjoyed at all you people planning my life for me," he said, "but one thing you can bet on, and make a note of it right now."

"What?"

"I'm not marrying Fanny Bannister. My mother is in on that, too. I'm catching hell from both directions. Sweetheart, if I take a notion just to ride out of here and find a job wherever I can, will you come along and marry me regardless of how your mother feels about it?"

She came to her feet and fell into his arms. Her lips parted for his kiss, and when he groped her body, she responded eagerly. But they both knew that this was not the time for it. This was merely a reunion, a declaration, a pledge.

"Let's put it in words," he said. "Eloísa, will you marry me?"

She was crying too hard to answer, but she nodded and seized his head to implant a passionately wild kiss on his mouth.

Not a man volunteered to stay and keep watch on the place for show night in Scobie. He had thought he could count on Shorty Gubbison, a reliable old man to whom he had delegated the job of finding a horse for Foster Bainbridge.

"Already found him, and I mean to ride him in and give him to Mr. Bainbridge that very night," Shorty said. "It's that sorrel gelding, Fox, that we worked on the light spring wagon for a while."

"Hell, he's only four years old and half broken, and he has never worked single," said Terence.

"You come with me."

Shorty had put shafts on the spring wagon. He put a breastband harness on Fox and took Terence for a ride. The horse was too long-legged to be called handsome, but he was gentle, deep-chested, and fast. He was, in fact, just the horse for the lawyer. So there went one hope. The way it looked, only a few aged and infirm Méxicans would be left on the place because most of them, over a hundred, had already arranged to go. Every team, every wagon and buggy and buckboard, was spoken for.

The big danger in leaving a place alone was always fire, but who knew what enemies Frank McNeil had made who would be saving their grudge's over who knew how many years for this very night? A man whose constructive avarice had remained operative until his ninety-fourth year and who had never fretted about double-crossing a friend anyway had enemies galore.

Ernest and Julia were still insisting at supper on Wednesday night that they were not going. Terence was pretty sure their minds would be changed for them by Uncle Frank, but if they remained, the need for watchmen would be that much more acute.

On Thursday there was a holiday atmosphere as the men buckled to their various jobs. He had never seen them work harder nor more cheerfully.

When he went in for the noon meal, Julia and Uncle Frank were resuming their old quarrel.

"At noon, one lunches," Julia said. "In the evening, one dines. To call this dinner and the evening meal supper is pure gaucherie."

"This is dinner, and tonight we have supper, and anything else is pure bullshit, Julia," Frank replied jovially. "You better be figgerin' what you're goin' to wear to the show tomorrow. We'll be leavin' right after dinner—or lunching, as you call it."

It should have been a merry meal, with Frank at the head of the table, Fanny at his right, Terence at his left, Julia next to Terence, and Ernest opposite her, next to Fanny. Fanny did her best to be entertaining. She had on a rather plain dress, one in which she could have done housework, and her hair was in braids wound about her head.

She spent the time cultivating Julia, who was unresponsive. Terence was glad when the meal was over, as Julia folded her napkin and sighed, "Beans, beans, eternal brown beans! What I wouldn't give for some seafood!"

"You can get awfully tired of that, too," said Fanny. "My father was a Boston fishing schooner deck hand, and often all we had to eat was what he brought home. We even got tired of lobster."

"I cannot imagine getting tired of lobster."

"That's because you've never been poor, Mrs. Orr. There were eight of us, and many a night we shared food for about four and went to bed hungry."

"You see, you ain't been so damn bad off," Frank said to his sister. "You'd complain if God set your table and had it served by the Archangel Gabriel."

"That is not humorous."

"Wasn't s'posed to be," Frank said. "Terence, you got the carriage cleaned up and two good teams picked out for it?"

"The carriage was waxed this morning, and it will be wiped down tomorrow. Who will be driving it?"

"Why, me, of course!"

"Well, I've got April and Bess on for leaders and Zack and Pesky for wheelers."

"Don't rightly remember that mare Bess, but I reckon you know what you're doing. Anyway, I kin handle 'em. Me and Ernest will ride in the front seat and Fanny and Julia in the back."

The old man could not handle four horses hitched tandem, especially four such steppers, but Terence knew this was not the time to say so. Uncle Frank would have his try at it and hand over the lines to someone else, but meanwhile he meant to terrorize everyone.

"If I'm dead, perhaps," Julia snapped.

"What about a horse for Foster Bainbridge? What are we going to tell him?" Frank asked, ignoring his sister.

"Shorty Gubbison picked out Fox, who used to work on the offside of the spring wagon. He's a jewel of a single horse and worth four times the horse that the lawyer lost."

"Gonna take him in with us?"

"Sure. Shorty will ride him in and throw his saddle and bridle in a wagon and come back with somebody."

"Knowed I could count on you, boy," the old man said affectionately. "Help me upstairs now, and I think I'll have a little nap. You might want to slip Shorty an extry five spot for a bonus."

It was a good idea, and Terence should have thought of it. He helped the old man upstairs, helped him remove his boots, and piled the pillows under him so he could sleep. Ernest came in just as Frank started to doze off and Terence to tiptoe out.

"It isn't healthy for you to sleep on a full stomach, Frank," he said. "You should wait at least an hour for your food to digest."

Frank was already too deep in sleep to do more than mumble resentfully, but he opened his eyes to glare at his brother. Terence took Ernest by the arm and slowly led him outside the room, with due respect for Ernest's cane. He closed the door behind him.

"Well, it's true," Ernest said. "Maria's got the top of his safe stacked with blankets and junk. Has anybody been in that safe lately?"

"I don't know and it's none of my business."

"It's mine, mine and Julia's."

"Take it up with Uncle Frank, but let him have his nap. Another thing—if you go to Scobie tomorrow, don't worry. I'll be riding beside the carriage, and if the teams become too much for him, I'll take over."

Ernest merely grunted. Terence steered him to the wide stairs and got him started down them, clinging to the banister with his right hand and leaning on his cane with his left. Terence himself took the narrow back stairs to the kitchen.

Pete Viscaino was clearing up around the back of the place with a scythe. He caught Terence's eye. "Don't worry about leaving someone to guard the place," he said. "I'm not going to the show, and I've got Marco, Pat, and Angelo at home for tomorrow night. Nothing's going to happen with us here."

"That's a big load off my mind. I'll give you a ten-dollar bill for each of them."

"Yes, and they'll tell me what you can do with it. They're doing this for me, not Frank."

Terence grinned. "I know how they feel, but tell them I appreciate it anyway."

Pete stopped to hone his scythe. "You carrying a gun tomorrow night?"

"No. Uncle Frank gave me one, and María was supposed to give me a holster and some ammunition for it, but why would I want a gun?"

Just then María came out the back door with some table scraps for the chickens. Pete spoke to her in Spanish. She went back inside the house and came out with the gun, four holsters, and a box of .45 ammunition in her apron.

"The señor says to pick out one that fits and shoot up a box every day. He says he told you about it. You are not to go unarmed anymore, Señor Terence."

The smallest and handsomest of the gun belts fit him best. He stuffed it full of twinkling brass cartridges and loaded the gun. It did not feel so heavy in his hand as he remembered.

"Better shoot it a few times today," Pete said. "Just in case you need it tomorrow."

"Why should I need it tomorrow?"

"Frank's got damn few friends in Scobie and none south of it that I know of."

Terence said to María, "All right, when Uncle Frank wakes up, tell him I'm shooting up one hundred cartridges. That's my job for the afternoon."

"*Bueno, muy bueno!*"

He knew that much Spanish, anyway. "*Gracias, señora,*" he said in reply.

He walked up the slope to the east until he was relatively out of hearing of the house, picking up a few tin cans from the dump. With the first few shots, he thought the gun would jump out of his hand, but he quickly got control of it. He walked several tin cans across the ground from fifteen to thirty feet before the afternoon was over. His hand ached, but not so badly as he had expected.

He looked over the carriage, which was not used more than once or twice a year. It was a handsome, expensive vehicle whose like was not to be found within a hundred and fifty miles. He looked over the harness to go with it and the teams that would pull it. For himself he chose a steady, reliable saddle horse with a handsome mane and tail.

Rather than let so fine a horse down, he decided to dress up a little for the show. He let Fanny pick out a shirt and pair of trousers for him and a scarf to wear in lieu of a necktie.

"It could be our carriage someday, and you wouldn't have to dress for the saddle," she reminded him.

They were in his room, with both doors open, the one to old Frank's room and the one to the hall.

"I'm afraid I doubt that a little bit, Fanny," he said. "I'm not the four-in-hand type."

"You don't know. You haven't tried it. There are so many things you haven't tried!"

"Yes, indeedy," he said. "Shall I give these to Maria to press, or will you? I've got work to do."

CHAPTER 7

Starting out to Scobie for The Show—so had Terence come to think of it—was like setting out on one of the straggling Crusades of the Middle Ages. The Méxicans got off first, in wagons and one hayrack, with a dozen riders. Overnight Ernest and Julia had decided to go, too, Ernest because he did not want to let Frank out of his sight, Julia because she was afraid to be left at home alone.

Then Frank decided he wanted the buckskins used as a lead team, and then he found his stiff and unsteady hands could no longer handle four lines. He sat in the front seat with Ernest, and Julia and Fanny sat in the larger and more comfortable seat behind.

"Goddamn it, Terence, you've got to drive. Ernest, you'll have to stay to home," Frank said.

"That's not fair. It's idiotic. Many a time six of us have ridden in this carriage," said Ernest.

"That was before they got as fat-assed as you are. You ride with somebody in the buggy."

"The buggy has already gone," said Terence.

Fanny leaped out of the carriage. "You just give me ten minutes to change to a riding outfit, and I'll take your horse, Terence," she said.

"He's pretty frisky."

"I'm a *very* good rider."

She ran into the house. Pete Viscaino helped Terence adjust the stirrups of the saddle. They both then had to help Ernest out of the front seat and into the rear to sit with his sister. Obviously Julia had not looked forward to riding with Fanny and was pleased, but Ernest was unhappy at having to ride in the rear.

Fanny ran out wearing a wine-colored riding dress with a split skirt and a wide sun hat with a veil.

She could handle a horse, no question about that. She checked the reins together in her left hand, and as the horse stepped backward in response, her foot found the stirrup and she was in the saddle, neck-reining the horse delicately.

Terence mounted to the seat and took the lines from Frank. The old man handed them over without a word, looking depressed and peeved. Every fresh evidence of advancing age, every loss of talent or ability, brought gloom to him. He said not a word except for curt, grumpy responses to Fanny all the way to Scobie.

The size of the crowd amazed Terence and somehow snapped Frank out of his depressed state. A huge green tent had been set up in the dusty, naked plaza, and tiers of green-painted benches had been erected under it. The four wagons and six teams that had hauled the show and its equipment had been stationed not far away. But the crowd so far overflowed the tent that its sides were already being raised on poles and tickets were being sold for standing room. There would, Terence estimated, be at least four hundred at this performance. And if they stayed overnight and gave the same performance again tomorrow, the same four hundred would be there to see it.

It was a happy, noisy crowd until the carriage appeared, flanked by its thirty riders. The Méxicans had already made camp with Méxicans from other ranches. Terence saw other men who obviously were cattlemen and proprietors because they gave Frank curt greetings, determined not to be awed by him.

To each he nodded. "Hidy, Louie. Hidy, Abe. Hidy, Fred, you ain't gettin' no younger, are you?"

"Neither are you," said Fred.

Frank grinned. "Hell no, I'm hell-bent to live to be a hundred. Onliest man in California born when George Washington was President. Terence, if they don't git out of your way, ride right over 'em."

The crowd immediately became surly, parted just enough to let the carriage pass. All eyes were on Frank McNeil, admiration vying with dislike and jealousy. You could hate his guts, but there was something about being ninety-four to which there was no answer. It was the same unwilling reverence, Terence thought, that Louis XIV must have seen in the faces of his subjects when the Sun King went abroad in his carriage surrounded by his armed and mailed knights.

They would spend the night with Foster Bainbridge, who had taken over what had once been a hotel with six rooms for rent. He used only three of them as a rule, but on occasions such as this he opened the other bedrooms to paying guests. This time, they would not be paying guests.

Foster came out of the front door to greet them. "Welcome, *bienvenidos*, nice to see all of you," he said. He recognized Fanny. "Why, Mrs. Bannister, what a nice surprise to see you!"

He gave her a hand down from her horse and handed the reins to a man, with orders to put it up in the stable back of the house. Other hired hands took the teams from the carriage. Bainbridge helped Julia down and gave the two women his arms to lead them into his house. Ernest, huffing and puffing, descended with only the aid of his cane, determined to show how hale and hearty he was.

But Frank put out both hands to Terence, and Terence staggered as the old man's weight came down on him. Bill Marquant, the resident deputy sheriff, strode toward them eagerly, taking off his hat and offering Frank his right hand. There were times the old man seemed to slip away from them into a faraway state of helpless senility, especially if he had exerted himself too much. He took the deputy's hand limply but did not speak to him.

Marquant was probably in his fifties, a man who had once been burly and powerful and tough but who was growing soft with the good life on the county payroll. He took Frank's other arm, and between them, he and Terence took the old man into Foster Bainbridge's living room, which once had been the lobby of the hotel.

Instantly Frank changed as he recognized the old room. He shook off their hands and made for the big rocking chair that Foster had had put here for him. He sat down with a sigh and stretched his legs.

"You're lookin' like you ain't missin' any meals, Bill," he said to the deputy. "How's the missus?"

"I lost her nigh three years ago, remember?" Marquant said gently.

"Oh yes. Sorry, Bill, but things slip my mind sometimes, and she was such a *good* woman, it's hard to think of the world without her."

The sanctimonious old bastard, Terence thought.

Foster Bainbridge came down the stairs, having shown the women to their rooms. Ernest was standing uncertainly in the living room, upset that no one was paying attention to him.

"Would you like to go to your room and lie down awhile, Ernest?" Foster asked him.

Ernest let Bainbridge lead him up the steps.

Without being asked, the deputy sheriff pulled a chair

close to Frank's rocker and sat down. "I was just talking to
Ruby Potter, and she's afraid there could be trouble here,
Frank. I wish you could keep your boys away from there
until, say, about sundown, and I'll make everybody else
leave then," he said.

"Why should my boys wait and take leavin's? They
won't start trouble," Frank said.

"They start it by merely being here. You haven't got a
friend south of your line fence among the cowmen, Frank,
and there's enough riders already come into town to wipe
your boys out."

"Where the hell did they come from?"

"What difference does it make? I just don't want any
shooting to start. I thought if you'd make your men turn
their guns in to me, I could make everybody else do the
same."

"That's a good idea, Uncle Frank," Terence said. "I'll go
with him and pass the word. We don't want trouble, not
with your sister and Mrs. Bannister here."

Frank's eyes blazed, but then he shrugged. "All right. I
reckon if anybody can get them to disarm, it's you. But
what if somebody refuses, what'll you do, fire him?"

"On the spot."

"All right, whatever you decide. I think I'll lean back
and take a little nap after Foster brings me a little liquor."

As Terence and Marquant went outside, Terence introduced himself, and the two shook hands. Marquant did
not quite know what to make of Terence, that was clear,
but he liked his ideas.

Ruby Potter's place was set in a grove of trees a block
and a half from the nearest building of Scobie, so hidden
among the trees that its size surprised Terence when he got
there. There were at least a dozen rooms built in a U
around the traditional patio, and this one was paved with

tile. Benches were spaced out on it with sunshades made of palm fronds brought all the way up from southern California.

Immediately Terence saw three Dot M Dot men. "There's a big crowd in town, and we want to avoid trouble, boys," he said. "We're all turning our guns in to Sheriff Marquant, here, so let's start with you."

The three gave them up reluctantly. Marquant buckled the belts so he could hang them over his left arm and led the way into Ruby's main parlor.

Ruby Potter was a tall, statuesque woman with black hair just going gray and a deep voice to match her decisive manner. She looked at the guns Marquant carried. "I see you talked old Frank into it," she said.

"Well," said Marquant, "his nephew, here, did. This is Terence McNeil, Ruby, and Terence, this is a woman whose word is as good as a government bond."

"All right, I'll pass the word; nobody comes in armed," Ruby said. She gave her hand to Terence. "Pleasure to know you. I've known your uncle for nearly thirty-five years, and he hasn't changed as much as you might think."

"I can believe that," Terence said.

They sat down to talk. She had four regular girls, Ruby said, but she had brought eight in for the show and the crowd it would draw. That meant eight who would be returning to San Francisco as soon as the show was over. "And I got only the best, Terence," she said. "The courtesy of the house to you, of course."

Before he could refuse graciously, she began calling her idle girls in and introducing them. "From this moment on," she said, "nobody comes in here wearing a gun. And if there's anybody in any of the rooms now with a gun, tell him as he goes out not to come back with it."

Terence and Marquant walked the town together, collecting guns. Now and then someone objected briefly but changed his mind when he saw the big pile of weapons the deputy was accumulating in his little office a few doors from Foster Bainbridge's place.

They came out of the house, after depositing another dozen guns there, to see two men tying to the limb of a tree down the street. Both were young, both wore guns, and both rode horses with the same brand, Streak of Lightning.

"Here's where we might have some trouble," Marquant murmured. "They work for Ed Mitchell, who used to own the whole ten thousand east acres of the Dot M Dot. Ed still carries a grudge."

He raised his voice. "Wait a minute, boys. Want to talk to you. Everybody's disarming today. No guns, with so many women and children in town."

"I don't reckon that goes for Frank McNeil's men, though," said one of the riders.

"Hell it don't. This is Terence McNeil, Frank's nephew, who manages the place for him. We're taking everybody's guns."

The young man looked Terence over with a puzzled frown. "That's a fact? I can't quite picture old Frank doing a thing like that."

"He didn't," said Terence. "I did."

"I notice you're still packing yours."

"Until everybody else has turned his in. Then Bill gets this one, too."

The man unbuckled his gun belt and handed it over. "I feel naked without it, but here it is."

The other man made no move to disarm. "I hear Baron Godfrey is working for Frank now," he said.

"That's right," said Terence.

"You got his gun?"

"No, I haven't seen him since we tied. I'll have it in half an hour."

"When you've got that son of a bitch's gun, you can have mine, not before. And when you see him, tell him that Slim Clarence is in town, and see what he does about handing over his weapon."

"Now, Slim, you don't want to make trouble," Marquant said.

"Put me in jail, then," the young man said. He turned and walked away, deliberately giving them his back, the gun swinging from his hip.

His friend shook his head worriedly. "I surely hope to God you can get Godfrey's gun away from him, because he'll kill Slim if Slim ties into him."

"You stay with your friend," Marquant said. "We'll go looking for Godfrey first thing, right now."

They pushed their way into the crowded livery stable, where several bottles were being passed around. It was a happy, hectic crowd with, Marquant whispered, not an ounce of brains in it. No sign of Baron Godfrey here. No one had seen him.

They walked through the corrals at the back without seeing him. They emerged on the side street, and Terence heard his name called. A girl was waving to him from the seat of one of the Dot M Dot wagons, where she was eating a *burrito*.

It was Eloísa, looking no more than sixteen in a vivid red blouse and black skirt. She was too far away from him to say anything, but he took off his hat and threw her a kiss. The Méxican children near her squealed with laughter, and she threw one back.

"There he is," Marquant said in a low voice.

Baron Godfrey came out of Foster Bainbridge's house, where, no doubt, he had been reporting to Ernest. Terence called his name, and the two walked toward each other, Marquant at Terence's side. Godfrey was dressed in new shirt and pants, and he had waxed and twisted his black mustache into sharp points. Terence had what he knew was an irrational dislike of men who wore such mustaches, and he had never seen Baron wear one before.

"We want your gun, Baron," he said. "Everybody's disarming. We don't want any trouble in such a crowd."

Godfrey shook his head. "Somebody just told me that Slim Clarence is looking for me to shoot on sight. Go get his gun first."

"No, I'll take yours first," Terence said. "Then he'll hand his over without an argument."

Again Godfrey shook his head. "It don't work that way with me. That smart little bastard has been making his brags about me for a year. I never threatened him none but I am now. If he pulls on me, I'll kill him."

"Goddamn it," Terence said, "give me your gun!"

Baron began backing away as Terence reached for his belt.

Across the street a voice yelled, "There you are, you cowardly, back-shooting son of a bitch. Go for your gun!"

It was the kid, Slim Clarence, walking stiff-legged toward them with both arms held out from his sides.

Baron said, "Slim, I ain't going to warn you again. Don't ever talk like that *to* me or *about* me, and keep your hands away from that gun."

But he began walking toward Slim with the same slow, stiff gait, his hands at his sides. When they were thirty feet apart, Terence drew his own gun and considered dropping a slug in front of each of them. In the military academy he had attended, such a shot would not have been considered difficult.

Incredulously he watched them march in silence until

they were no more than eight or ten feet apart. Incredulously he watched Slim Clarence grab at his .45 and get it out. It was no more than half raised when Baron Godfrey's hand darted down. He was cool, relaxed, and fast—oh, so fast!

He shot Slim Clarence in the chest and then in the face before the kid could even get his gun up. He shoved the gun back in its holster and turned to face Terence and Marquant, raising his arms.

"You seen it and heard it," he said. "He made me draw. He pulled first."

"But you knew you could kill him," Terence said.

"Sure. But he was the one making the brags. I tried to warn him."

The street was suddenly full of a hundred men, and at least twenty of them had seen the shooting.

Terence walked up to Baron, swallowing his rage and making an effort to keep his voice calm. "But it wouldn't have happened if you had handed over your gun when you were told. The McNeils will see you through this because it was a form of self-defense. But the minute the inquest is over, you're fired."

"Inquest? What the hell you talking about, inquest? Everybody seen him draw first."

"We don't usually hold inquests on something like this," Bill Marquant said diffidently.

"You do this time," said Terence. "There'll be no talk that a bastard who works for us shot a man *that he knew he could kill* and the law did nothing about it. Just for the records. Then I'm going to run Godfrey out of the country and—*no you don't!*"

Godfrey has started to reach for his gun again. They were less than six feet apart. Terence jumped him and swung at his jaw. Baron twitched his head aside, and

Terence caught him in the throat. He knew then that the man couldn't box.

He sunk a left into Godfrey's belly and then another one. He threw a right cross to the jaw that dropped Godfrey to the ground, unconscious. He leaned down and snatched the gun from Godfrey's limp fingers and handed it to Marquant.

"Somebody's empowered to conduct an inquest, and I'd bet a dime it's you," he said. "You start getting the witnesses together, and when this bastard comes to, put the handcuffs on him. I'll go report to Uncle Frank and then come back and be your first witness."

"I reckon that's the best way to handle it," Marquant agreed. "I don't like to have to sign my name to something without testimony."

Terence went into Foster Bainbridge's house. His uncle was asleep, Foster said, and to awaken him now with news of a killing might have bad consequences. But he agreed with Terence that an inquest was in order and that Bill Marquant, the only representative of the law here, was the man to conduct it.

"I'll volunteer as his legal adviser during the proceedings, and I've got a fast writer who can take down the testimony," he said. "That's using your head, Terence. Without an inquest, within a week it would be all over California that Frank McNeil's man murdered this fellow in cold blood."

The handcuffs were removed from Baron Godfrey's wrists before the inquest began in the outdoor shade of the grocery store. Godfrey still wore a dazed look, as though he could not understand what had happened and was happening. A young man who was reading law with Foster took the testimony down, and Marquant read from a book to swear the witnesses as they were called.

Terence was first, and his testimony took no more than twenty minutes. Subsequent witnesses took only three or four minutes each, since all they had to testify to was that Slim Clarence had drawn first.

The jury of six men that Bill Marquant had chosen stepped aside to confer. In a moment they called Foster Bainbridge to come to them and advise them. He talked to them a moment and handed them a paper that he had already prepared. Each signed it. It declared that the deceased had met his death while making an unprovoked attack and that the act of killing him was one of self-defense to which no criminal taint was attached.

"I don't know what that got you," Baron said to Terence. He was still suffering from a sore jaw and talking with difficulty, but he was getting some of his old arrogance back.

"It didn't get me anything," said Terence, "but it saves Uncle Frank's reputation. I'll pay you to the end of the month, but you be out of this town within thirty minutes."

"I want to see you make that good after I talk to Ernest."

"Let's go!"

Terence took the man by the arm that had drawn the gun that killed Slim Clarence and walked him rapidly down the street to Foster Bainbridge's house.

Frank was awake and having a sandwich and a cup of coffee in the dining room. Ernest was still asleep. Foster had followed Terence and Godfrey and was present when Terence reported what had happened.

"What do you want of me?" Frank demanded peevishly. "You said you was going to fire anybody that didn't give up his gun. Well, do it!"

"I want to see Ernest first," Godfrey said. "If you please, Frank, I got a right to see him. He's always been my friend and—"

"You never had no friends," Frank said. "How much do we owe him?"

"I told him I'd pay him to the end of the month. That'll be thirty dollars."

Frank merely gave Foster Bainbridge a look. The lawyer got three ten-dollar bills and a book of receipt forms from his safe.

"I ain't going to sign one of them damn things," Godfrey said, "not until I talk to Ernest."

"Then you don't get paid but you still get the hell out of town," said Terence.

Godfrey signed. He took his money and folded it into a wallet already fat with currency. He snatched his hat up from the table where he had laid it and walked out and went stalking up the street. Foster sent a boy to tell Bill Marquant to see that he left town, but the boy could not have been gone three minutes when they saw Godfrey canter up on his horse and haul it down in front of the house.

"I got all my clothes at the place. I got a right to them," he said.

"Sure," said Terence. "Come around tomorrow between one and two, and you can have everything that's yours. Get this, Godfrey—I'll be there personally to go to the bunkhouse with you and get your duffle. And then you're on your way."

The man hesitated and then turned his horse and rode off, favoring his sore jaw by the way he held his head.

When Ernest came down, Frank told him, with no little glee, what had happened to his favorite.

"Every hired hand I ever liked, you managed to get rid

of him," Ernest said. "You don't want me to have a friend on the place."

"That's right," said Frank, "I don't. The kind of friends you pick, you might as well pick a yellow dog. That's all Baron Godfrey was—your sneakin' yellow dog."

Ernest gave Terence a long, spiteful look. "I shall not forget this, Terence," he said. "I know who is responsible. You'll regret this!"

CHAPTER 8

The show was excellent, much better than Terence had expected. He sat between Julia and Fanny, and Fanny told him that Darryl Means had assembled a company and taken to the road to get Orlena out of New York and heal an incipient consumptive spot on her lung. How Fanny knew this, he had no idea, but he did not doubt that it was true.

The spirit of the crowd was more than receptive; it was prepared to enjoy and appreciate everything. And that was something to figure out, too, after what had happened this afternoon. Perhaps they felt more confident now that they had proof that gunplay would no longer be tolerated and that the Dot M Dot would enforce discipline on its own men.

Someone had seen Baron Godfrey riding out of town not long after the coroner's jury had cleared him. He had on his gun, but as he rode, he rubbed his right wrist as though the handcuffs had been locked too tight on them.

"That man will try to make trouble for you," Fanny said to Terence when Baron's name was mentioned. "I don't have to tell you the sneak's part he has been playing."

He did not commit himself; he did not trust her not to capitalize on gossip, trading a bit here for a bit there, building up a knowledge of something that was none of her business.

"He's a man-killer," Fanny went on, snuggling closer to

him and lowering her voice. "They say there used to be many like him around here, but today he's an anachronism. But of course Ernest wouldn't see that, or wouldn't care."

"Well, the only thing I have to worry about is when he comes to pick up his clothing and collect his pay, and I think that will be pretty simple," Terence said diplomatically.

The Méxicans occupied their own section of the audience, and he quickly picked Eloísa out of the crowd. If she was watching him and Fanny, she gave no sign of it. She had two little kids in tow—probably the children of relatives—and was buying them peanuts and spun sugar candy.

At the end of the show, after Orlena Means had taken encore after encore on her full, rich, true-toned whistling, her husband announced that the show would stay over and appear again tomorrow night. Then he paid his little tribute to old Frank McNeil, who sat squarely in front of him, five rows back, in the best seat in the house.

"Before we say good night, I want to state that the entire company is proud and privileged to have appeared before a man who is a distinguished historical character, Mr. Frank McNeil!" he said ringingly. "We are all a little closer to the history of our country tonight. Mr. McNeil is ninety-four years old, born when George Washington was President, and has made himself one of the leaders of this glorious, growing state."

There was considerable applause, although Terence noticed that Ed Mitchell and his five or six men did not join in it, nor did some of the Méxicans. Frank grinned and tottered to his feet with Terence's help. He waved his response but did not try to say anything. The people parted to let the Dot M Dot contingent through, first Frank, with Terence and Fanny on either side of him, followed closely by Ernest and Julia.

They spent the night at Foster Bainbridge's house, and as usual it was mostly a sleepless one for Frank. He kept Terence up talking far into the night. "You should've brought your fiddle along," he said. "That's what I need, something to relax me and take me away from the cares of the day."

"Well, we can't turn another man's house into a night concert chamber, Uncle Frank," Terence said.

"Foster wouldn't mind. I noticed there was a big organ in a corner of the dining room. Go wake Foster up, and ask him if the goddamn thing works."

"I don't like to do that, and I'm not much of an organist anyway."

"That's right, give me an argument every time I ask a little favor of you. Foster would like to hear it played himself. He bought it for his wife, and nobody has ever been able to get music out of it since she died."

Terence got up wearily and went to the lawyer's bedroom, which he was sharing with Ernest. He had not gone to sleep yet; Ernest had kept him awake complaining for an hour and a half now.

"So far as I know, it's in perfect condition, and I would take it as a privilege if you would try it, Terence," he said. "I'll call one of the boys to pump it for you."

Ernest was grumbling louder than ever as Foster slipped into his pants and went out to arouse one of his men. It was a young Méxican who plainly had pumped the organ before. He opened all the stops and took hold of the big hardwood handles to pump the dust out of it. Meanwhile Terence had discovered a stack of sheet music in the big bench, mostly Bach and Handel.

It was going to be a struggle, and Bach and Handel would probably do handsprings in their mausoleums, he thought as he sat down and fingered the two keyboards. He started with Bach's "Jesu, Joy of Man's Desiring" because he knew it and it was one of Frank's favorites as well as his own.

It was a splendid instrument that gave him confidence. It filled the old hotel with melody such as it had never heard before. Upstairs Ernest began thumping on the floor with his cane, demanding silence, but outside the street had filled with people, mostly Méxicans. Close to the door he saw Eloísa.

He had his nerve with him tonight. He dared to improvise and play by ear. He played two more Bach pieces and then, holding a high, flutelike note diminuendo, he segued into "La Paloma." He knew that it was a classical Méxican folk song and that he was probably butchering it by playing it by ear this way, but they went wild when he had finished.

Julia, wrapped in a quilted robe, came downstairs barefoot. "Can't you hear Frank hollering at you?" she snarled. "He wants you to play "La Panchita." He'll never go to sleep until you do."

"I've never heard it."

From outside the door Eloisa cried, "I know it! If I can hum or sing it and you listen, can't you try it?"

He smiled and nodded, and she began to sing. He knew enough Spanish by now to know that this was a song about a somewhat naughty Panchita, and the tune was a simple one in the rather mournful Méxican tradition. He quickly picked it up, increased the volume, and soon had the whole crowd in the street singing with him.

He played for an hour, at which time Fanny came down to report that Frank had gone to sleep. But as the crowd broke up, as Terence started back up the stairs, the old man awakened.

"Why'd you stop playing? Jesus Christ, first time in ninety-four years I ever heard organ music, and you deny me this," he said.

"Uncle Frank," he said, "I'm not really playing. I'm faking half of the harmony."

"All right, if that's the way you feel. I like that Méxican music. Git that girl, Eloísa, in there to help you. She knows all the old Méxican songs."

Eloísa came in gladly and stood with her hand on his shoulder, proprietarily, as he played. Now and then she stopped him. "No, no, no, it goes like this," she would cry and begin singing while he tried to follow with a thin, low melody.

Never once, to judge by the reaction of the crowd outside, did he fail her. Desire for her thickened in his throat, and by the way her fingers strayed softly over his shoulder, he knew that she was moved in the same way. They dared not look each other in the face. Julia had gone upstairs, but Fanny was still here, watching and enjoying everything but their obvious intimacy.

It was after two-thirty in the morning when he finally closed the instrument. "Thank you so much," Fanny said, rising. "This was an unexpected ending to a very joyful evening, Terence."

She blew him a kiss and ran upstairs. Terence walked Eloísa to the door and then, instead of letting her out, closed it with her inside. His arms went around her; she melted against him lithely and parted her legs so he could caress her. How the hell, he thought, am I going to work this?

Foster Bainbridge came in and caught them in a writhing storm of passion, she leaning back over his left arm with her whole lower body exposed to his roving hand. She gave a little cry and straightened up and wriggled within her black skirt.

"There's a little bedroom off yours and Frank's, and no one ever need know you're there," he said. "Come, I'll show you the way."

At breakfast the next morning Frank, feasting on a fried beefsteak with fried potatoes, said how well he felt and how deeply he had slept. "I'd like to deal you out of that organ, Foster," he said. "I don't want to take it if it means that much to you, but if it's for sale at any price I want it."

"An organ is meant to be played," said the lawyer, "but I couldn't accept anything for it. The horse you gave me to replace my old bony friend is worth more on the market than the instrument."

"An organ," Ernest said. "A noisy organ, bellowing like a bull half the night. Where would you put it, Frank?"

"I don't know. That's up to Terence. He knows about things like that." He looked at Terence. "In the livin' room, do you think?"

"Yes, on the south wall where the bookcase is now," said Terence.

"Sure, right under my room," Ernest said.

"Ernest, I rather liked it," Julia pleaded. "Just because an organ *can* bellow doesn't mean that it must do so all the time. Maybe Terence can play some church music on it, too."

"Hell yes, anything that's music," Frank said. "A thousand dollars, Foster, is that about right?"

"It cost me less than half that fifteen years ago."

"But you bought it from somebody in San Francisco that went broke. I remember now. Will you take a thousand dollars and not feel yourself cheated too bad?"

There were times when you could not refuse the old

man, and this was one. Frank sent a man to hire a stout
dray wagon and six men. The wagon went with the procession that started back to the Dot M Dot, the organ se-
curely roped in place in it. Some of the Méxican kids
wanted to ride with it, and suddenly Eloísa snatched several of them by the hand and helped them in. She sat in
the back of the wagon, which had no endgate, dangling her
bare feet.

The cowboys waited until the procession was ready to
start and then rode on ahead of it. In the lead was a top
buggy driven by Shorty Gubbison, with Ernest beside him.
Then came several wagons, loaded mostly with Méxicans,
and then the wagon with the organ. Behind it Terence
drove the carriage, with Frank beside him and Julia and
Fanny in the back seat. There were several other wagons
stretched out behind them.

Fanny talked animatedly, in a holiday spirit and with
cozy little references to things that only she and Terence
could share. She played the piano; she could teach him the
harmony of the left hand. As she said it, "bass clef" became somehow an erotic term that only they understood.
Terence, Eloísa in sight and her face and body etched forever on his mind, courteously kept up his end of the conversation.

They were halfway home when they saw two men riding
hard toward them from the ranch. Both, Terence recognized, were Dot M Dot men and Dot M Dot horses. They
passed the leading rigs and the organ and pulled their spent
horses down beside the carriage.

On their faces were identical looks of awe, of horror, of
something he could not place. "Like to talk to you a minute in private, Terence," one of the riders said.

Frank had been dozing, but he came wide awake now.
"Private, hell! What's eatin' you two?"

Reluctantly the man said, "There's hell to pay at the ranch. Pete Viscaino is dead in the front yard, shot three times with a heavy rifle. His son Marco was shot in the head from behind, I think with another rifle, near the back door."

"Pete and Marco shot? What the hell for?"

"Somebody busted into the house and blew the door off your safe, Frank. The Viscainos caught them. They scattered papers all over the hell. We've sent to Merced for the sheriff, but a blind man could see that Pete and Marco interrupted a burglary. Anything valuable in that safe is gone."

"Wasn't nothing valuable in it. Just some old papers. Who the hell would want to burgle it? How the hell did they blow it open?"

"I don't know. Just blowed the whole door halfway across the room. It nigh fell through the floor into the living room."

"It was a real old safe. Any good burglar with an ounce of nitro could blow the door off. But why? By God, I don't like this a bit! Step it up, Terence, and let's get there."

Terence put the teams into a trot and went around the wagon that carried Eloísa and the organ. Word spread rapidly up and down the Dot M Dot procession, and Terence could only hope that it was not some wild fiction that would panic everyone or, worse still, inspire a blood lust for vengeance.

He mentioned the messenger close to him. "Did anybody see anything of Baron Godfrey?"

"No. Never thought to look for him, but he's sure not around there."

"He ought to be. He was sent home last night."

The man scowled and thought it over, shaking his head. "That son of a bitch," he finally said in a soft voice. "If he shot them Viscainos from behind, hanging's too good for him."

They saw the crew lurking around the outside of the place, morosely keeping their morbid watch. Terence had a man take the carriage around to the other end of the house so the women could enter by the kitchen door. He dismounted and went to kneel beside Pete's body.

"Look," one of the men said, "he hasn't got no rifle, and there's not a spent ca'tridge in his forty-five. One through the chest that would have killed him, one through the back of the neck that would have killed him, one through the belly that would have killed him a little slower."

"Meaning?"

"First shot got him in the belly and dropped him. That's why I think Pete had a rifle, because they didn't dare come any closer then. They finished him off before he could spot them and bring his gun up, and then they took the rifle and went around back to deal with Marco. Look, I'll show you."

They went around behind the house. Marco had obviously been watering his horse because it was still tied by the reins at the nearest tank. He had probably heard the gunfire and started running toward the house. He got within thirty feet of the back door when a heavy rifle slug, fired from the corner of the house where the smokehouse stood, had drilled him in the back. He probably had not even twitched after he fell, since his spine was severed. His .45 had not been touched.

"No other dead men?" Terence asked.

"No. We looked everywhere."

"I had better get the old people inside and break the news to them. One of you go to the bunkhouse, though, and see if Baron Godfrey's stuff is gone."

Julia became hysterical and at first refused to enter the

house. Fanny finally persuaded her by sending in for a bottle of whiskey and a glass. Ernest seemed stunned, unable to grapple with what had happened. It was a tribute to old Frank that he kept his head.

They went inside and up to his room. The door of the big iron safe had indeed been blown off and halfway across the room. Terence had heard that if nitroglycerine could be used to fill the crack between the door and the body of a safe, held there by soap, and ignited by a primer, it would perform exactly this way. But it took a professional burglar to do it.

"The goddamned sons of bitches," Frank said. "Wait until we're all gone, and then come in and do this."

"What were they after, your will?" Ernest quavered.

Frank grinned. "If they was, they didn't get it."

"But you always said it was in the safe."

"Sure I did, hell yes, but that damned old pile of soft iron could've been opened with drills and a crowbar. No sir, that will is safe where nobody is going to find it! And there wasn't no other valuables, just keepsakes and deeds and stuff, and the deeds is all recorded, so they wouldn't do nobody no good. Call María to get some women to start picking this trash up."

The Méxican women came up and gathered up the papers. Among them was a faded tintype of a man and a woman, and the man was plainly Frank McNeil. On the back was the date, October 18, 1846. Terence handed it silently to Frank.

"Me and Martha, my second wife," he said. "I forgot I had this. Took in San Francisco when I took her up there to see the doctor. She never came home. Cancer."

Indifferently he handed the picture back. There was a sheaf of old letters on strange paper, several from Lydia, his first wife, whom he had married in 1814 and who had died four years later at the age of twenty. Frank himself would have been twenty-four or -five then.

"You can take all that stuff outside and burn it, Terence," Frank said. "It's so fur in the past, it don't mean nothing to nobody now."

"It ought to be saved for its historical value, Uncle Frank. Let me keep it and sort it out and turn it over to the historians."

"No! I don't want them snoopin' through my private affairs. Burn it, I said."

"Damn it, Uncle Frank, when one is as old as you are, you have no private affairs."

Baron Godfrey's things were gone from the bunkhouse. So was the Winchester 73 that had hung just inside the kitchen door. Both bits of news were brought as Frank and Terence were sorting and stacking the papers from the safe as the Mexican women gathered them up.

Julia had retired to her room and bed to calm herself. Ernest was in his room, too, but he was moving about noisily. He came to the door while the messengers were still there after bringing the news of Baron Godfrey.

Frank narrowed his eyes and stared at him with cold fury. "I don't suppose you know anything about this, Ernie," he said.

"About what? This murder and burglary?"

"Yes. 'Pears it was your man Godfrey done it."

"You don't know that. That's just spite speaking. Why would he do anything like this?"

"He'd kill the Viscainos because you told him to, and he'd find a burglar who could blow the door off because he'd know exactly where to look for one."

Ernest sat down heavily on the bed. "Baron is gone?" he quavered. "He's not here?"

"No. What did you ever say to him about what's supposed to be inside that safe?"

"Nothing! Nothing! I won't stand for this. The idea that I would hire someone to kill and rob—you're out of your mind, Frank."

"Maybe you're the one that's out of his mind."

Ernest rubbed his face with both hands. "If Baron did it, he did it on his own and *he* is out of his mind. But it's still your fault, Frank, making a game out of tantalizing everybody about your will. If Pete and Marco are dead, you're to blame for that, too. Go ahead, kick me out. I don't care! I'd rather starve on the roadside than tolerate any more of this."

"I ain't going to kick you out, Ernest," Frank said. "I wouldn't think of it, no sir! I want you to be here when we bring Baron in. I want to hear the two of your together."

Ernest leaned his forehead on his cane and sobbed brokenly.

CHAPTER 9

The Viscainos had already been notified. Angelo was in the bunkhouse; Patricio remained with his mother. "Go see him, Terence," Frank said. "Tell him I'll pay for the funerals, I'll give his mother a thousand dollars, I'll put up some kind of memorial at their church. It's down near Scobie somewhere, a country church, you know the kind. They always need everything."

Before Terence could reply, Julia spoke up with some spirit. "Stop and think a minute, Frank. The least you can do is give Renata back her land and go tell her about it yourself."

"*Her* land?" the old man shouted.

"Yes, *her* land. You and she used to be friendly. Her husband was murdered in your service, probably by one of your men. So was her eldest son."

Frank glared at her a moment. "I'd have to give them an easement across my land to get from that place to the highway. It's worth ten times as much as it was when I had to foreclose on Pete. You're crazy!"

"Then I have no more to say." Julia folded her hands in her lap and looked away angrily.

"Terence," said Frank, "go see Angelo, and tell him what I said to tell him."

Terence stood up. "I'll tell him, but I'll tell him what Julia said, too, and I'll tell him that I agree with her. I won't be a party to any tightwad compensation like that for the deaths of two men like Pete and Marco."

Frank seemed to ready to choke on his own rage. "Then somebody help me up and give me an arm, and I'll go tell him myself. Or tell him to come here."

"Uncle Frank, he has already been asked here," said Fanny Bannister. "He won't set foot in this house. He says he understands the bodies have to lie there until the law gets here, and he's going to stay to see that they are not molested, but he doesn't want to see you."

Frank stopped struggling to get to his feet. "Honest to God? Why—why, I gave that kid his first pony! I gave him his first gun, an old Colt Peacemaker. He used to call me Uncle Frank."

"He won't anymore," Terence said. "Uncle Frank, you've got to think a few things over, but I'll go talk to him anyway."

He went out to the bunkhouse and found Angelo Viscaino seated in the dining room, talking with the cook and a couple of Dot M Dot cowboys and eating big hunks of hot, freshly baked bread and drinking black coffee. He looked like Marco, just as darkly bearded and curly-haired, but he was slimmer. He wore a Colt .45 on his hip.

"I know who you are," he said when Terence started to introduce himself.

"Then I want to know what we can do."

"You've already done enough. Not you. I know that you tried to lay the whip to Godfrey, and I don't blame you. I just want to know what you're going to do about hanging him."

"First we've got to catch him, Mr. Viscaino, and we've already sent to Merced for Sheriff Hall. It's his move."

Angelo did not meet his eyes. "Omar Hall is all right, but Bill Marquant is twice the man Omar is at something like this. One of your boys has already gone to bring him. And when Godfrey's caught, I want to twist his arm until I find out from him what your uncle had to do with this. Ernest, I mean."

"I want to know that, too, but I'm sure in my own mind that Ernest never had anything to do with the planning of this."

"You're a hell of a lot surer than I am. Listen, I want to talk to you alone a minute."

At a glance from Terence the cook and the sympathetic cowboys left the room. Terence did not wait to be asked to sit down. He took the end of the long bench across the table from Angelo. He could see the stricken, helpless look in Angelo's eyes and the tamped-down rage that he was holding under such strict control. He had a feeling that under other circumstances, Angelo would be easier to like than Marco had been.

"What can I do, Mr. Viscaino?" he said.

"What's Fanny Bannister doing here?"

The question startled Terence. "Why, just visiting, is all. It's all I know, anyway."

Angelo snorted. "Then listen to this! She and Baron Godfrey lived together in San Francisco for several years."

"What!"

"Frank don't know it; but they did. It was right after her husband died and left her all that money. Baron moved in and helped her blow it, and then she kicked him out. That was four or five years ago."

"This is a shocker that I find hard to believe."

"I can prove it. Now I ask myself why Baron came to work here for cowboy's wages. He's got quite a bit of money laid by of his own. He couldn't help but know that that crazy old Frank was sweet on Fanny. And I'll tell you something else, Baron was a spy for Ernest from the day he hired out here."

"I'm sure of that, but as far as Uncle Frank being sweet on Fanny, he's been nudging me to marry her myself."

"Sure, what the hell could a ninety-four-year-old man do for her? Just make sure that nobody outside of the family got her, and leave her all his money. This is the first time he's seen her in several years. Now just when he's made a will leaving everything to you, she turns up."

"Leaving everything to me? Nobody knows what's in that will, Angelo. I certainly don't, and I don't think it leaves very much to me. I've been the old man's poor relation, is all, the son of a brother so much younger than he that he barely remembers him."

Angelo glowered into his cup of cold coffee. "Well, you can kiss it all goodbye now. Fanny will get it, and she'll give Baron Godfrey any amount to get the hell out of the country. Or hell, she might even marry him! She hated his guts for a while, just before her money ran out, but who knows about women?"

They were interrupted by the arrival of the priest, who was disturbed by the fact that the two bodies had been left out in the sun with nothing but a pair of bedsheets to cover them. He knelt and said a prayer over each. His name was Father David Pohl, his church was Santa Margarita's, and he was withdrawn if not downright antagonistic to Terence.

Deputy Sheriff Bill Marquant arrived a few minutes later on a winded horse. He was accompanied by Orrin Bailey, one of the performers in last night's show. Bailey was a big-framed, taut-muscled man in his forties who had served for ten years with the New York Police Department, most of them as a homicide dick.

Between them they had already learned a few things.

Marquant's first question was, "Yesterday was Baron Godfrey riding his own horse or a Dot M Dot horse?"

Terence said, "I didn't notice. Every man here has a string of two or three. I know that Godfrey has a horse of his own, but I couldn't even tell you what it looks like."

Several of the riders who had gone to the show yesterday said that Baron had been riding his own bay gelding with black feet and mane. Marquant and Bailey had found several places where the horse had been tied, not hard to do, since Godfrey was a loner described as "a man who never tied with the bunch." His horse had been shod on all four feet.

Bailey had sketched tracks of the horse. The bay had big feet, and the shoes were old and needed replacing, so they left distinctive marks. The left rear one was short a nail. He was slightly pigeon-toed in front, often the sign of a fast-walking horse with a long stride in his hind legs. A good horse, a tireless horse, but sometimes hard to handle, those who knew him said.

The horse was now missing. So was a pair of saddlebags belonging to another cowboy. No one had been found who had seen Baron Godfrey after he had ridden out of Scobie after being freed by the coroner's jury. He had apparently ridden straight to the Dot M Dot, an easy half hour's ride. How he had approached the place and what had happened then were the questions.

Then it occurred to Terence that he would have had to get inside the house to get the Winchester from the kitchen. The Viscainos would not have questioned him if he had simply ridden straight up and said he was running an errand for Ernest—or for Frank, for that matter. And sure enough, there were the horse's tracks where he had been tied to the circular bench around the pepper tree behind the house, where Ernest so often sat.

They could even see boot tracks, no doubt Baron's, lead-ing to the back door. He had stopped and turned once, probably to shout and explain himself to Marco up at the horse tank, and then had gone on into the house.

Once he had the Winchester in his hands, he had slipped through the house to the front door. No doubt Pete Viscaino had come on foot toward the house to inves-tigate his presence. He was probably twenty feet from the *pórtico* when Baron slipped on through the house to the little-used door at the other end of the *pórtico*, in an extra bedroom.

He had opened the door carefully and snapped a shot that caught Pete in the abdomen. It would have been a fatal shot, but Pete would have been good for a shot or two before he died. Thus, Baron had taken the time to shoot twice again.

Marco had come running down the back slope, hearing the heavy triple boom of the rifle. Probably Baron had raced out of the house, closing the door behind him, and gone around the end of it, taking the path Ernest used to the bench under the pepper tree. One shot was all it took because it severed Marco's spine and lodged in his chest cavity.

"All right," said Marquant, "we know who we're looking for and how he's armed and what he's riding."

Sheriff Omar Hall got there about then. He might not have been the criminologist that Marquant and Bailey were, but he was a good sheriff who supported his men. He was an old McNeil retainer, and although he wanted to talk to Frank, when he heard that the old man was taking a nap, he agreed to wait.

"What about this fellow Godfrey killed in Scobie? Find out anything from his buddies?" he asked.

Marquant had talked to two friends of the dead rider.

All they knew was what the late Slim Clarence had told them. Slim had had a crush on a girl in a brothel in Stockton about a year and a half ago. She had told him how Godfrey had abused her and of the indignities he had expected of her. But by the time the kid went looking for Godfrey, he had quit his job and moved on.

"They said that Godfrey always carried a wad of bills as thick as the end of a wagon tongue. He wasn't no ordinary hired rider, although he was a damn good stockman and rider. Good gambler, too. And they was both surprised to learn he had been working here for thirty a month for so long. It just didn't seem like Baron Godfrey to them."

The whole Dot M Dot crew fanned out to look for the tracks of Godfrey's horse until darkness. The only sign they found was where a horse had crossed a sandy blowhole about five miles north of the house on Frank McNeil's range. But the sand did not hold clear-cut tracks, and the best anyone could say was that it *might* have been Baron's horse.

The sheriff returned to Merced to have some Wanted posters printed and put in the mail. A team was hitched to a low-bed wagon with a straw tick and a quilt on it, and the two bodies were put in it to be taken to the Viscaino house and from there to Santa Margarita's, five miles to the south. Terence went up to the side of Angelo Viscaino's horse just before the cortege left.

"I want to come and talk to your mother and brother," he said, "but I can't agree yet with Uncle Frank on what I can say."

Angelo's swarthy, bearded face remained expressionless. "Reckon you got different idees on what's due to the family."

"More or less."

"Terence, I hear nothing but good about you, but I

don't think this is the time to talk to Ma. She never did for a minute agree with Dad about him workin' for that old man."

"I can understand that, and I wish she knew it sometime."

"What're you going to do about that goddamn Fanny Bannister?"

"I'll know more about that when Uncle Frank wakes up."

Angelo nodded and unexpectedly put out his hand. Terence took it for the briefest of handclasps and then stood watching the wagon, with its mounted escort, lumber across the slopes toward the land that once had been Pete Viscaino's. Before it went out of sight, he turned and went into the house through the kitchen door.

María was just cleaning up the lunch dishes for the family. It was not necessary for her to say she had not called him because she knew he was busy at more important things. She asked him what he wanted to eat.

He shook his head. "I have no appetite now, *gracias*, María. Maybe later."

"La Señora Bannister is waiting for you in the living room. She wants to talk to you while Señor Frank and Señor Ernest and Señora Julia are asleep."

He went into the living room and found Fanny wiping down the big organ, which now dominated the room. Upstairs all was silent, but the remains of the big iron safe lay in the front yard, and the skids on which it had been brought downstairs were still on the steps. He could not help smiling a little bitterly to himself; when it came time for Frank's nap, nothing got in its way.

"Hello, Terence," Fanny said, putting down her dustcloth. "Did María tell you I would appreciate a moment or two with you?"

"Yes. Why don't you sit down? I think we have a few things to clear up before we go any further."

Her face told him that she knew he knew about her and Baron Godfrey. Who on the ranch would not have heard it by now? She retained control of herself, only a slight pallor indicating a certain inner tension.

"I'm too nervous to sit. I pace things out. I wonder what you're thinking of me now."

"I'm wondering why we never heard anything about the relationship you once had with Baron Godfrey."

"Why should you? It was not something I was proud of. My husband left me a business worth more than forty thousand dollars. Baron went through it in three years."

"How do you happen to know Uncle Frank?"

"Believe it or not, through your mother. Elena and I were very close. I idolized her as so many young girls idolize older, prettier, more sophisticated women. It was she who introduced me to my husband. He was a good man. When he died, your mother knew Frank had an office in San Francisco then, and she wrote and suggested that I go see him for advice about my future. I did, only I didn't take it. I met Baron Godfrey instead."

He said nothing. She went on earnestly after a moment. "I was much younger and stupider and more impressionable than I am now. I blame myself, and yet it was something that could have happened—*did* happen, I found out later—to wiser women than I. Women will always want to be victimized by a certain type of man, and men generally despise that kind of a man."

Terence remembered Baron Godfrey's waxed mustache and understood. "If we catch him—and I think we will—I don't think there will be any trouble proving he committed these murders. He'll hang for them."

"I hate hanging, but he should."

"Where would he learn how to blow a safe the way this one was blown?"

"I don't know, but he knew how, all right. He worked with another burglar in San Francisco; I know that much because I had to hide them after they almost got caught burglarizing a shipping office."

"What did he want from Uncle Frank's safe?"

She looked surprised. "Why, his will! For years I've been his principal heiress. He told me himself that I would be worth half a million. Then you came along. He never told me any differently, but he told others that he had located a nephew and was making him his sole heir. A few bequests to María and the Viscainos and so forth, but you would get everything else."

"Fanny, I simply don't believe that."

"You can believe it. Just last night I asked him about it. A woman can say things like that to a man that another man couldn't. He said if you and I got married, he would leave everything to us in joint tenancy. Otherwise I'd come out of it with the same as María, ten thousand dollars and a hundred a month the rest of my life," she said scornfully.

"The brutal old bastard," said Terence.

"The brutal *rich* old bastard," said Fanny. "I suppose it is useless to suggest that we go ahead and get married. I know you're in love with Eloísa, and I would never embarrass either of you over that."

"I'm afraid I don't believe that. No woman is going to live the rest of her life in that position."

"I have lived in much worse."

Suddenly she walked toward him and put both hands on his shoulders. She slumped against him and let her arms creep up to encircle his neck. He heard her draw several heavy sighs that were almost sobs and then felt the pressure of her breasts and body against him.

She could not help but feel his instinctive physical reaction, but he did not give in to it. Gently he disengaged her hands and arms and stepped back, shaking his head. "I told you before that it's not for me," he said as kindly as he could. "You can have Frank's goddamn money. I don't want it."

"You mean you don't want me. You want Eloísa."

"I suppose it comes down to that."

"But, Terence, there is no way I could get Frank's money if you turned it down. I'd still get only ten thousand dollars. The rest would be divided among a hundred friends and relatives. It would be twenty years before it was all settled and anybody got anything."

"Even if the new will were destroyed and the old one became the valid one?"

"The new one is not destroyed, but the old one was when the new one was signed. Frank told me that himself. He doesn't mince words. He actually *giggled* when he said I'd have to get you to marry me to get a half interest, otherwise it all went to you."

"Where is the new will?"

"He said only Foster Bainbridge knew that, and Foster had it fixed so even if they tortured him to death, he couldn't betray the will."

"So Baron committed double murder and burglary for nothing."

Her quick, hot flush of passion had subsided, leaving her face cold and a little older-looking. "Yes, and I warned you yesterday, he could make trouble for you. If he comes back in the middle of the night, it'll be to kill you."

"What good would that do?"

"You made him stand for an inquest. You had him handcuffed. You fired him in public. And Ernest would file a suit claiming a brother's share of the estate of an incompetent, and he'd have to pay Baron or it would all come out. He hates you, and you have no idea how he can hate!"

CHAPTER 10

Every peace officer in the state had copies of the posters that made Baron Godfrey a wanted man. Terence had asked Frank about offering a reward. "At least a thousand dollars," he said. "That's enough to smoke out most people, but fifteen hundred would be better. That will turn his own friends against him."

"I don't care. Whatever you think," Frank said. "You all seem so damn sure it was him that done it and that you can convict him."

"Uncle Frank, it couldn't have been anybody else. If he's still riding the same horse when he's caught, the district attorney says it will be easy to convict him, even if the horse has been reshod."

"All right, I ain't arguing. I'll put up the fifteen hundred," Frank said irritably.

The sum of fifteen hundred dollars was enough to make every peace officer greedily vigilant of strangers. The San Francisco chief of police had a special squad of three detectives working on that case alone. But as far as anyone could tell, Baron Godfrey had vanished from the face of the earth.

The brutal murders had taken years off Julia Orr's age. She was still cranky, quarrelsome, and bossy, but she was no longer querulous and vague. She seemed to make her peace with her older brother, and she and Frank spent long hours together talking over their long-ago childhood. She still disapproved of Frank's long daytime naps, which kept him awake in the night and cost Terence so much sleep, and the sound of the violin still enraged her. But she was more tactful about it in her comments.

Ernest, on the other hand, seemed to slide over the brink into senility in a single day. Physically he was probably healthier than before, because he hobbled about the place on his cane, getting more exercise than he had in years. But he talked to himself, had trouble focusing his mind in conversation, and had to be tended by Julia at mealtimes. She filled his plate, cut up his food, and peppered him with instructions: "Don't eat so fast. Use your fork, not your spoon. That coffee's too hot, Ernest; wait till it cools. No, you mustn't have any more beans. You know how they gripe you."

Ernest coldly ignored Terence until the last day the workmen were there cleaning up after repairing the damage done to Frank's room. It had been decided to leave the four supporting posts for the safe standing in the living room because it was easier than taking them out, but Frank's windows all had to be replaced and studs and siding in one wall strengthened.

Terence stopped for a moment to watch the carpenters at work overhead. Ever since childhood he had always liked watching an artisan who was good at his trade. He became aware of someone behind him, and before he could turn a voice murmured, "The old order changeth. Who said that? What's it from?"

It was Ernest, not the old Ernest, because his wits were still muddled. But a pitiful sort of peace had come to his face, and his searching eyes invited Terence's forgiveness. Terence impulsively put his hand on Ernest's arm. The old man smiled gratefully, mumbled something, and moved on. It was as though he was making his moments count for something that was important to him, now that he was running out of moments.

Frank stayed out of the room while the men were there, only requiring them to get out for two hours each afternoon while he took his nap. They drew their wages for sitting in the shade of the pepper tree out back, dozing or gossiping.

One afternoon Terence rode into the back yard and spoke to the workmen as he dismounted and tied his horse.

The carpenter foreman was an egotistical little Irishman who called nobody mister. "As soon as the old man wakes up," he said, "we've got about an hour's work, Terry, and then we're ready for our pay."

No one had ever called him "Terry," and he was not sure he liked it. "What did you do with the junk from the safe?" he asked.

"Throwed the iron on the junk pile yander," the Irishman said, pointing toward a gully where they had been using junk to stop erosion for years, "and knocked the brasswork out and sold it for a dollar. I reckon you figger you're entitled to that."

"No, it's not worth—" Terence started to say.

Julia appeared at an upstairs window, her eyes immense in a pallid face. "Terence, oh thank God you've come," she called softly. "Come up here. Take your boots off and don't make any noise and hurry, hurry!"

She was gone before he could question her. Terence ran into the house. María and one of her helpers were working in the kitchen. He asked them what was bothering Señora Julia. Neither knew that anything was bothering her. He stepped out of his boots and took the stairs two at a time in his sock feet.

Julia came out of her room and clutched him. "Sh-h!" she hissed. "It's Ernest. He's in Frank's room, and he's got a big pistol, and he's waiting for Frank to wake up so he can kill him."

"The damned old fool, where did he get hold of a pistol?"

"Oh my God, what difference does it make? In this jungle you can find one or two in every room. Go take it away from him before he does something terrible."

"You stay here. I may need your help."

He went into his own room and cautiously, inch by inch, opened the door into Frank's. Frank lay sleeping soundly on his back, propped up on his pillows as usual. Ernest was not visible. Terence opened the door a little wider.

Not ten feet from him Ernest sat in a rocking chair with his back to Terence. The Colt .45 in his hand was barely visible. He rocked gently and seemed to be having trouble staying awake. But he also mumbled to himself, his voice soft but the words quite distinct. "I've waited for this a long time, Terence, but I shall not kill you in your sleep. You may have one minute to face your crimes, and then— boom, you're dead! What have you done with my brother, answer me that? Where is Frank? I know you, Terence McNeil, whether anyone else does or not. You cannot disguise yourself from me."

Curiously, Terence felt more pity than fear or hostility. The poor old fool with the gun too big for him thought that his sleeping brother was Terence in disguise. The walking, breathing, eating part of him lived on, but his brain had died. He was an irresponsible child, flitting from one emotional peak to another without rhyme or reason.

Terence took a backward step and a look down the hall, where Julia was nibbling on her handkerchief and fighting to repress her sobs. He tried to reassure her with a smile. He motioned her: *Stay away and be quiet!*

He opened the door a little wider and raced on silent tiptoe to the rocking chair. The damned old fool even had the gun cocked so that the lightest pull would discharge it. Terence threw himself across Ernest's lap and closed his hand around the gun so that if the hammer fell, it would fall on the web between his thumb and forefinger.

He jerked the gun out of Ernest's hand and lowered the hammer. Ernest merely stared at him with his mouth open for a moment.

"Give me back my revolver," he said then with offended dignity. "That was a present from Frank when the model came out, and those cartridges are smokeless powder."

Frank awakened, as he always awakened, without a start but with a complete realization of time, place, and surroundings. He sat up in bed. "What in hell is going on here?" he demanded.

Ernest pointed a trembling hand at him. "You can't fool me. You're not my brother! You're Terence in disguise. You've killed Frank, and you'll kill Julia and me, the same as you did Pete and Marco, too."

Frank looked at Terence. "What the hell is he talking about?"

Terence shook his head. "He's a little confused. I'll explain later." He raised his voice. "Aunt Julia, it's all right. Can you come help get Uncle Ernest out of here?"

"You'll explain later hell," Frank said, throwing back the covers and planting his big, bare feet on the floor. "I want to know what you two are doing in my room with a forty-five."

Julia came in and tried to get Ernest to rise from the rocking chair, but he angrily and stubbornly resisted. Terence carried the gun across the room to Frank and handed it to him.

"Did you give this to your brother?"

"No, what gave you that idee? This is a brand-new gun. I don't think it's ever been fired."

"You gave me that in eighteen seventy-eight, and later you gave me smokeless powder cartridges for it. For my birthday. Let's see, it was my seventy-ninth birthday."

"He's right, you did, Frank," said Julia.

Old Frank examined the gun carefully. "By God, I did at that. This gun never was worth a damn. The cylinder wouldn't lock. Where have you had this tucked away, Ernest?"

"It has always been in my dresser drawer, the top one, where I could get at it in an emergency."

Frank grinned at Terence. "Good thing he never tried to fire it. Take it out and get rid of it somewhere. What was he doing with it here?"

"I'll tell you later."

"You'll tell me now!"

Terence merely shook his head and helped Julia hoist Ernest to his feet and hand him his cane. Ernest let Julia lead him out of the room. Terence closed the door behind them.

"Julia caught him in here waiting for you to wake up so he could kill you. He thought you were me in disguise, Uncle Frank. He thought I had killed you and was pretending to be you," Terence said.

Frank handed him the gun. "Get rid of it, and see that he don't get his hands on another one. Old fool is getting childish. Tell María to bring me up a cup of hot coffee and help me get dressed."

Half an hour later, Frank came downstairs. Terence was working at the books at the desk in the corner behind the four posts. Frank yawned and went to his favorite rocker and sat down.

"Hotter than hell," he said. "Come talk to me. What're you doing?"

"I've tried to get a count of every head of livestock on the place. There's a lot that should be sold off while the price is up."

"Ain't got enough to use up the grass I got. Let 'em run wild and multiply."

Terence closed the book and put the pen aside. "If you insist, but that's a damn poor way to run a ranch. A lot of this stuff—both cattle and horses—will never be worth this much again. I've penned up nearly eighty broomtails that I'd like to auction off wild, just to get rid of them."

"All right, suit yourself. Ain't had an auction sale here in a long, long time. What do you figure eighty ought to go for?"

"I'm not that good a judge, but some of the boys are, and they say they'll run anywhere from ten dollars to a hundred dollars apiece. Say an average of sixty. That's forty-eight hundred, less advertising and the auctioneer's fee. We could round up a few more and probably net out five thousand."

"I'll think about it."

The old man began a rambling discourse on a horse he had bought at a wild horse auction in Sacramento in 1874. Best horse he had ever owned. While he was talking, Fanny Bannister came into the room. He forgot all about his horse to greet her with a smile and stroke the hand she offered him. To Terence it was plain that he would have liked to caress her more intimately.

Suddenly, still clinging to Fanny's hand, Frank turned to Terence. "Play us something on the organ. You haven't tetched the damn thing in two weeks."

"I've had too many other things to do, Uncle Frank."

"Oh wait, Uncle Frank, I found some music in the bench I'd like to hear him play," Fanny cried.

She opened the bench and took out a stack of sheet music over an inch thick. On top was a waltz, "The Artist's Life," by Johann Strauss. Excitedly she put it on the music rack and ran to the kitchen to ask María to send someone in to pump the organ.

She then had to stand beside him, most of the time with her hand on his shoulder, to point out the fingering of the left hand. Terence quickly caught the spirit of the piece and had no trouble with the lilting melody.

"Let's play it as a duet," Fanny said. "You play the upper keyboard and invent your own harmony, and I'll try to follow you with the other keyboard."

Surprisingly it was a success, especially with Frank. To share the small bench with Fanny was slightly unnerving to Terence. Her light perfume, a flower scent, seemed to become stronger and stronger. It seemed to him that the pressure of her hip against his was unnecessarily heavy. He was extremely conscious that he was squeezed against an aroused and extremely desirable woman who was having trouble keeping her mind on the music.

She gave up suddenly, snatching her hands back and looking him in the eye. Her face was flushed, and her mouth trembled. I'm just not musician enough for you," she said. "Maybe Uncle Frank would excuse us to go take a ride."

"All right," Frank said, "but you two practice that tune every day, you hear me? That's one of the purtiest tunes I ever heard."

"We'll try to work on it," Terence said. "But I haven't got time today for a ride, Fanny. I've got a crew working."

She caught his arm and squeezed it. "They don't need you. Please!"

He excused himself again, firmly, and went out and rode up the slope to where his men were patrolling a barbwire fence that enclosed the eighty wild horses. Shorty Gubbison had ridden through the herd several times and now was of the opinion that they were probably worth a little more on the market than they had originally estimated.

"Net out five thousand easy, Terence," he said. "They's some damn good horseflesh in there. Sell off the broomtails first for what you can get, and then the bidding starts."

And here came Fanny Bannister, in her wine-red riding habit with a wide-brimmed straw hat held by a cord under her chin. The men eyed her bouncing bosom hungrily. She could ride well, and the horse was a stepper, and hers was the kind of lush figure that showed to best advantage in the saddle.

"Are these the horses you want to sell?" she asked. Terence nodded. "Can I talk to you about them?" she went on.

The men took the hint and left them alone. Some of the wilder colts simply refused to believe that a strong, five-strand barbwire fence could deny them freedom, and a wild stampede could have left some of them badly wire-cut. The men rode among them, breaking up the groups that might panic, letting the horses learn the hard facts of life about barbwire one at a time.

"Will they really bring in forty-eight hundred dollars?" Fanny asked.

"Better than five thousand, I think."

"When can you have the sale?"

"You've got to have about a month to get your advertising out. It has to be printed and mailed to every horse broker and livery barn you can think of, and the auctioneer will have his own list."

She bit her lip. "You couldn't do it in two weeks?"

"Not very well. Why?"

"Uncle Frank will let me have the money; I know he will. And oh God, Terence, you can't imagine how much I need it!"

"Fanny, if he wants to give you five thousand, he doesn't have to wait for a horse sale. He can get it from a dozen places."

She shook her head. "You don't know him if you think he'd do that."

"Some things are just impossible, and setting up a big auction sale in two weeks is one of them."

She met his eyes boldly. "Forget it. Come for a ride with me. There's something I want to show you."

He could have said "I can't," but it would have done no good. It would only have deferred whatever showdown she had in mind. He waved his hat at Shorty Gubbison—*take over*—and followed her on up the slope. She let her horse take a fast pace, sitting erect in the saddle so that he had her shapely rump in view all the way.

She said not a word. She ignored him entirely until they had climbed up to where scrubby conifers grew in the edge of the pine zone. She pulled up then and let him catch up with her. She still said nothing, but the blush on her face and the rapid, gusty breath that came from her parted lips told him all he needed to know.

"I rode up here the other day," she said at last. "There's the most beautiful canyon, and I saw a mountain lion streaking across above it. Just a flash and it was out of sight, but how thrillingly beautiful it was!"

"And we rode all the way up here to see that?" he said, not quite smiling.

"Just wait."

The forest became more dense; dogwood and alder throve in between the pines. They rode most of the time now in shadow. Suddenly she pulled her horse down in the bottom of a small, flat canyon that was completely surrounded by trees. She slid from her horse and held it by the reins.

"Get down. I'll show you what I mean," she said breathlessly.

As he dismounted he tried to remember Eloísa, but could not recall her face.

Fanny pointed up the slope. "I was sitting right here when my horse spooked," she said. "I saw the lion streaking, just streaking like lightning, across that knoll there. You see that clump of brush with the whitish leaves? He dived into that and was gone."

She closed her eyes. "It was like suddenly being in a wild, free world where you could do anything you wanted and it would be good and beautiful. Civilization was a million miles away. Can't you feel the same thing?"

"In a sense, I suppose so. It was one of the sensations that first reconciled me to staying here—the feeling that everything around me was new and fresh and wonderful."

"Then you do know." She handed him her reins and stepped close to him and began unbuttoning her shirt.

He got control of himself and said, "Cut it out, Fanny. You're a very desirable woman, but I'm a very bullheaded man."

"How can you make fun of me when I want you so badly?"

"I'm not making fun of you. I'm just not the man for you."

"You are, you are, I know you are!"

He narrowed his eyes. "Fanny, what has this got to do with the five thousand dollars you need?"

"Uncle Frank will let me have it if you tell him to, and I'm offering you all I've got if you'll do it."

"Uncle Frank doesn't take my advice. I can speak to him. I'll really try to get him to give you the money, but you don't need to do this, and I can't arrange the sale in less than a month."

"I need the money in two weeks. I've got to have it!"

"For Baron Godfrey?"

He might as well have hit her on the jaw. She went limp and pallid, and he had to catch her to keep her from collapsing on the ground.

"Fanny, if you have any idea where Baron Godfrey is you have to tell me. I wouldn't give you a damn nickel, I wouldn't even shake hands with you to help him."

"You don't know him," she said. "You just don't know him."

He said nothing. He would have given her a hand up on the horse, but she mounted expertly without his help. The horse wanted to go, but she held him there another moment.

"I truly do need the money," she said, "but even without that I wanted you to make love to me. All right, now anything that happens is your fault. Just remember that when the time comes."

He snatched at her horse's bridle and held it. "When what time comes?"

She heeled the horse in the ribs. He let go of the bridle, and she headed for home. He swung up into the saddle and went after her. She ignored him when he caught up and rode beside her. Plainly she was not used to being rejected by a man, plainly she had a strong appetite for love and a man's blunt attitude toward it, and just as plainly she was in terror of Baron Godfrey, wherever he was.

Which meant, to Terence, that Baron was not far away. They avoided the holding pasture where the wild horses were being assembled for auction and came down to the back of the house without encountering anyone else. Ernest was sitting on the circular bench around the pepper tree, leaning on his cane and dozing. He opened his eyes when he heard them.

"Hello there. Have a nice ride?" he asked.

"Very nice, Uncle Ernest," Terence said.

The old man seemed to be completely unaware of the episode in Uncle Frank's room with the .45.

The woman dismounted. Terence slid out of the saddle and said, "Give me your horse. I'll put him up for you."

She handed him the reins. "Thank you," she said coldly.

"And about that other, you think it over, and let's see if we can't swap information so I can get you that money for your own use, not for him."

She compressed her lips and shook her head. "You're a fool," she said, and started for the house.

Uncle Ernest watched her until she went in the kitchen door. "Lovely woman, lovely woman," he said. "I knew her husband. He didn't deserve her."

"Who was he, Uncle Ernest?" Might as well learn all he could while the old man's mind was functioning.

"He had a little money that he loaned out, and he had to foreclose a tannery south of San Francisco. He decided to run it rather than sell it, and he made a very good thing of it."

"I see."

"He was murdered, you know. Throat cut and robbed of nearly a thousand dollars. They never did find out who did it."

"Were they happy while he was alive?"

Old Ernest shrugged. "There was talk about her, but I don't remember the details. It was said that she—but I don't carry gossip. But if her husband had lived two more years, he would have had a chance to leave her a wealthy woman. That's just how well that tannery was going."

"Uncle Ernest, how did you happen to meet Baron Godfrey?"

"That's very simple. He came to work here. Frank hired him. He was very kind to me."

"Why?"

A blank, secretive look crossed Ernest's face. "He was very kind to me, that's all. To everyone else I was just a parasite, an old fool living off Frank. Baron treated me like a man again! You won't know what that means until you're my age."

"Did he ever mention Fanny Bannister's name to you?"

Senility descended over Ernest's face like a mask. There was actually a physical change that made him look, not just old, but foolish and helpless. He tried to take a cigar from his pocket, but he fumbled it and let it fall. Terence picked it up, unwrapped it, and lighted it for him. The old man puffed away contentedly, staring at nothing. Terence was sure that Ernest did not even know he was there.

CHAPTER 11

Years ago Ernest had taught María to play cribbage to pass away the dull evenings. He quickly lost interest in it as she learned to beat him, but for years Frank had had her in two or three evenings a week. They were well matched and could play three or four hours without losing interest or without either one gaining much of an advantage.

Terence had no idea how María interested the old man in resuming the games, but she did, and they served two purposes. They gave Frank a new interest in life, something to look forward to as the summer came to an end and the evenings grew longer. And they reduced the demands on Terence to find ways to amuse his uncle.

He spent at least one of these evenings each week with Eloísa, which had been María's principal design. She wanted them married, but if that never came to pass, she wanted her daughter to better herself and be happy. If she married another Méxican, even in *unión libre*, she would become part of the ranch's Méxican community, her position there fixed for life.

Old Frank McNeil had always liked Méxicans, had learned their language, had protected them from exploitation by other *gringos*, had been godfather to numberless of their children and had given each a birth gift of money. And yet it had never occurred to him to help them change their way of living. The men who worked as cowboys got the same pay as his other men *if* they lived in the bunk-house and remained single.

But if they married and occupied one of the *casas*, they were expected to support their families and to accept as gifts from the *patrón* what thirty dollars a month would not buy. As Terence's wife, Eloísa would break out of the confines of the *barrio* forever. Even as his wife in free union, she would be better provided for and their children would be entitled to use the name McNeil.

Eloísa and Terence had firmly settled that they would marry; the only question was when. Eloísa was philosophical about it. She was happy with him this way; why fret over dates in the future? The downtrodden learned to wait, even as they hoped, and both María's and Eloísa's calendars were adjusted to *tiempo Mexicáno*.

"You're not like yourself tonight," she said to him the night after the episode with Fanny.

"Something is wrong. What?"

"I can't get it out of my head that Baron Godfrey is somewhere close by, ready to hit again," he said.

"What makes you think that?"

He told her about his ride with Fanny. "He's trying to extort a lot of money out of her in a big hurry, and when I ask myself how, all I can think of is that forty-five he killed that kid with in Scobie and the Winchester forty-four that used to hang in the kitchen."

"There are not many places he could hide, not and hide his horse, too."

"There has to be one. I think he may have given her a deadline. Either she comes up with the money, or he kills somebody else. Not her. Me, perhaps, but more likely Uncle Frank."

"Why him?"

"It would throw the will into probate court and tell him exactly who is to get what."

"Have you looked for him anywhere?"

"I've looked for him everywhere. Honey, I never ride out alone anymore because I want my back covered against that Winchester. There isn't a shanty, a cave, a camping place I haven't explored."

She put her palm on his cheek to kiss him. "The thing to do," she said then, "is to send for Pancho."

"Who is Pancho?"

"*Pancho de los Leones*. He's an old man who makes most of his living tracking and hunting *pumas*, what you call mountain lions. He and Señor Frank are not friends, but for my mother he will do it."

"Do what?"

"Meet you and talk to you and track down Godfrey if he's anywhere near. If you can tell him what kind of track to look for. Maybe even if you can't. He will not want Señor Frank to know he is helping, and he will demand much money from you, maybe even fifty dollars a month. That's what cattlemen pay him when a *puma* becomes a calf killer."

"It's a deal. How do you get in touch with him?"

"I'll ask Mamá. She'll know how, but she'll want to know why you want him."

"Tell her. Fifty a month is dirt cheap. Tell her to get word to him to meet me somewhere. I can show him drawings of the horse's tracks with the old shoes on. He may have new shoes by now, but they say he walks pigeon-toed in front and has a long hind stride."

"You don't have to tell me these things, *corazón*. Tell them to Pancho. There is something else I want to talk about now."

"What?"

She moved into the circle of his arms and kissed him with a stirring passion.

Pancho of the Lions turned up four days later, meeting Terence just off the road halfway to Scobie. He did not offer his hand but in his soft voice said, "There is nothing on earth I would do for Frank McNeil, but María says you are different, so I'll see if I can be of help to you."

"There's also fifteen hundred dollars reward up, you know," Terence said.

The other shrugged. "By the time the sheriff and his deputies and all the others take their share, what is left for me? I know how this business works." He was an old man, white-haired but still wiry, strong and active, and intelligent and better-educated than Terence had anticipated. Pancho of the Lions was a loner pursuing an isolated trade, but he was not uncomfortable in the presence of another man. He had his own dignity.

"If you track him down," Terence said, "I'll personally guarantee that you get two thirds of the reward. A thousand dollars, even if I have to make it up myself."

"I would not expect you to do that."

"I'll do it, and I can raise it. Pete Viscaino was a friend and a man I respected. This is a personal matter with me."

"Pete and I were friends for fifteen years, too." Pancho nodded toward the .45 on Terence's hip. "I know this Baron Godfrey. Can you shoot that gun? He is a crazy man who enjoys killing."

"Any man who kills and enjoys it is crazy."

"Agreed."

"I can handle this gun far better than he can his, far better than you may think." Pancho looked skeptical, so

Terence went on, "Most of these famous gunfighters, I understand, made their reputations at point-blank range. I learned to shoot in a military school—thirty, forty, fifty feet. He's not going to get close enough to me to take that advantage away from me."

Pancho still looked skeptical. He pointed to a scar on a stunted cottonwood where a branch had been pulled off and the bark had tried to grow over the mark in the trunk. "That's about thirty, thirty-five feet, Señor McNeil. How close can you come to that?"

Terence snatched out the .45, thumbing back the hammer so he could fire it like a single-action gun. He squeezed off a shot that made his horse jump under him and saw bark fly from the cottonwood less than eight inches from the scar. He holstered the gun and brought his horse under control.

"That's close enough to knock him down. I've got him then, and that's as close as he'll ever get."

Pancho nodded. "Good shooting. María said you had some pictures of the tracks of the horse he rides."

"Drawings, of the one he did ride. We don't know that he still has the same horse."

He unfolded the sheet of paper and handed it to Pancho, explaining the horse's distinctive gait. Pancho studied it a moment and then handed it back. "I will know those tracks if I see them, even if he has had the horse shod again."

"Won't you need that to keep?"

Pancho raised his eybrows. "Why?"

"You say you know him. When last seen, he had a dude's waxed mustache twisted into points."

Pancho nodded and thought it over. "There is something you ought to know. There is a woman staying at your house, about thirty, very pretty, with yellow hair, and she rides well."

"I know. Fanny Bannister. What about her?"

"It was about two weeks ago she met a man at the old Martínez cabin. Know where that is?"

"Yes. About a mile down the road but about a quarter of a mile east."

"Yes. It was none of my business, but I think it was this man, Baron Godfrey. She had a flour sack full of things tied on behind her saddle. She did not get off the horse when he took the sack off. He patted her behind, and she hit him across the face with the ends of her reins. She hurt him, too. Anyway he dropped the sack and covered his face with both hands. And then she rode away. I think I'll check the Martínez place and see if they have been back."

"You don't think he'd be living there?"

"No chance of that, but they could use it as a meeting place."

"Any reason I can't go with you?"

"All right with me."

Most lion hunters hunted with big packs of dogs. Pancho had only two: huge hounds, one a bitch with a starchy aggressiveness to her and jaws like a blacksmith's vise. Both came at Pancho's soft whistle and followed behind them to the Martínez cabin.

It lay on Mitchell ranch property and for years had been used by wayfarers as a place to rest for the night. Mitchell had kept driving them out and had let the old shanty fall to pieces until it was no longer used by anyone. Pancho dismounted a good fifty feet from it. Terence did likewise.

The grass grew right up to the door of the cabin, but the long summer had dried it out, and restless, waiting horses had killed most of it. The dogs coursed the cabin two or three circuits and then lost interest; they were lion trackers, not horse trackers. But Pancho found imprint after imprint that could be identified as the tracks of Baron Godfrey's horse. The worn shoes still had not been replaced.

A little chill went through Terence as he thought of the tempting flesh of Fanny here alone with Godfrey. Or maybe that was what she wanted. On the other hand, she had slashed him across the face with her reins for taking liberties that were no longer his. One thing was certain: There was probably very good reason for her urgent need for money, because Godfrey would need getaway money now, not later.

Pancho promised to scout the country and parted with a cordial nod and a *buenos días*. On his way back to the Dot M Dot, Terence cut down to the highway. On trees and fence posts he saw where the auction ads had been freshly tacked. He hoped that Godfrey saw them, too, and would leave Fanny alone. The auction was only two weeks and two days away now. Lord, Terence thought, give Godfrey patience.

Men were daily visiting the ranch to look over the horses to be offered for sale. Some of them Frank invited to supper. One, an old-timer, a mere seventy-five years of age, exclaimed over the big organ while they waited in the living room to be called to dinner.

"My nephew plays it," Frank said proudly. "Same boy I'm training to run this place. That kid can do anything well."

"That's not what he tells me when we're alone," Terence said to the guest.

Frank grinned his ugly old grin. "I give him plenty of hell. Yes I do. But I got another guest, a lady, who helps him out on the organ. We'll ask them to play for us after supper."

Terence had avoided Fanny since meeting Pancho, and she had apparently avoided him. So far as he could tell, she never left the place. She went for her daily ride but was never gone more than half an hour. She spent most of her time in her room, embroidering a cape for herself. They had not exchanged more than a dozen civilized words since that incident in the canyon where she had seen the mountain lion. He could still remember the contempt in her voice when she said, "You're a fool."

She joined them at dinner, wearing a dress that he had seen often but that was attractive enough to draw lavish praise from the old visitor. She brightened immediately. She was lonely, Terence knew, with only Aunt Julia for company, and she was one of those women who needed the constant reassurance of praise and courtship. When Frank asked her and Terence to play the organ after supper, she gave Terence the warmest smile he had had from her since before that rebuff.

"We haven't practiced together for a long time, Uncle Frank," she said, "but we'll try our best, won't we, Terence?"

The two boys came to pump the organ. She sat down beside him sedately enough, but he could tell when the physical contact between them that neither could avoid began to arouse her. The strange thing was that she played better for it; whereas he lost confidence and with it the touch that made him like his own music. They played "Artist's Life." They played "Jesu, Joy of Man's Desiring," she playing a barely audible counterpoint that Bach would have approved of. They played "Listen to the Mocking Bird," and while he carried the melody, she played the bird songs that seemed to fill the room with their actual presence.

But in an hour she abruptly tired of it. She excused herself and went out. Terence sat and talked with Frank and the horse buyer, who would spend the night here in one of the guest *casas* outside. When Terence got up to excuse himself, Frank pointedly looked at his watch.

"It's early. How about a little cribbage?"

"Afraid not, Uncle Frank. It's not my game."

"I bet I know what is," Frank said with a lewd grin. The guest, too, excused himself and went out, yawning, to his bed in the little guesthouse. Frank squinted at Terence. "Why go outside the house for it? Fanny likes you."

It was time to have it out with him. "Listen, Uncle Frank, are you trying to fix something up between Fanny and me?"

"You could do a hell of a lot worse."

"Why? What do you care?"

The old man's mind had never seemed keener. He scowled, drumming on the tabletop with his big knuckles. "Time you and me had a little talk. Set down."

It was Terence's turn to consult his watch. "I haven't got time for a long talk, Uncle Frank."

Frank chuckled his deep, guttural chuckle, as obscene as a dirty story told in a pool hall. "This won't take long. She'll wait. What the hell else has she got to do?"

"That's the whole point. I don't want to treat her disrespectfully. Not just because she's your granddaughter, not just because she's a Méxican, but because she's a lady."

"Where'd you hear she was my granddaughter?"

"Oh hell, Uncle Frank, everybody knows it." He sat down at the table, putting his hat on it beside him. "Her grandmother was good enough for you. Why isn't she good enough for me?"

"I didn't marry her grandmother, either. She's a lady. You're right there. But you don't have to marry her. The

Méxicans have a different way of looking at things. The plans I've got for you, it might be a good thing if you had kids by three or four Méxican girls."

"What do you plan to do, stand me at stud?"

Frank laughed, then abruptly sobered. "You might need all the kinship support you can get from the Méxicans in time. I changed my will sometime back. You know what I'm worth? Besides this ranch, I mean, and it's good for two hundred thousand any day. Well, there's another nine hundred thousand in shares and bonds in the vault in a San Francisco bank."

Terence caught his breath. "My lord, that means you're a millionaire."

"Yes, and I didn't get it by giving it away. What's this I hear about you keeping Wes Peterson on full pay, with him laid up with a broken leg?"

"He's not entirely laid up. We splinted it, and it's healing, and we made him a crutch, and he's doing a lot of useful work. He was hurt working for you, Uncle Frank, and it's the least you can do for him."

"Any man got hurt or sick on the job here, I always kept him on and took care of him. But I don't pay a man for doing nothing. That way you end up with a bunch of crips and invalids. Minute a man knows he's got something wrong with him, he comes here and hires out if that's the way you run things."

"I'm sorry, I disagree. I wouldn't cut off Wes Peterson's pay."

"Well, it's coming out of your own pocket in the end. I'm leaving everything to you. I've set up a trust fund of two hundred thousand so Fanny will get ten thousand cash and a hundred a month, and Ernest and Julia will get a hundred a month, and so will María; and when she dies,

Eloísa will get it. But what's left when they all die goes to you."

Terence was not surprised, but it still left him confused and a little breathless. "Why, Uncle Frank? I'm not a cattleman, and we've been strangers most of my life."

"Money should stay in the family, and who the hell else is there besides you? The way you took hold here, why, it just cheered me up more than you can imagine. I expect to live to be a hundred, and by then you'll be the best damn cattleman on the Sierra slope. And tell me this, what good is a Méxican wife going to be then? Her grandmother, Josefina, got fat and bad-tempered by the time she was forty. She couldn't even read and write. She raised our son, Javier, up to be a worthless mama's boy."

"What has that got to do with Fanny Bannister?"

"I've always liked Fanny, and she's older than you, and she knows the value of a dollar. She'd be a big help to you. Times is changing. Style's going to count more and more, and a man in your position is going to need a wife who can trot in any harness."

"I'm afraid she has already trotted in too many harnesses for me, Uncle Frank."

The old man waved a hand irritably, dismissing the subject. "She was married, sure. But that's good experience that you need. And she likes you."

"She likes your money."

"And you don't."

"Not that much." Terence stood up and reached for his hat. "I came here broke, and I can leave here broke if it means marrying a woman I don't want to marry."

"Why don't you want to marry her?" The old man suddenly flew into a rage. "She's like my own daughter. I ain't going to partition this property, or I'd leave her half of it.

But I plan on you two getting married so she can be mistress of the place. You can have Eloísa and a dozen more in *casitas* and it won't make any difference. But when it comes to a wife, it's got to be somebody proper for the position."

Terence leaned on the table and looked his uncle in the eye. "Like Fanny, right? Did you know that she's Baron Godfrey's old lady friend? And that she's still tangled up with him some way? Has she asked you for five thousand dollars?"

"No, and she—"

"She will, and it'll be for him. She's keeping him fed from your pantry. He's got something on her that makes her help him."

"That's a goddamn lie!" Frank bellowed.

"Wait until after the auction; see if she doesn't hit you up for the proceeds. I don't blame her. I feel sorry for her, and I like her, but not enough to marry her just to make sure she gets a half share of your property!"

"Baron Godfrey—why, she wouldn't spit on him!"

"Ask her. Or just tell her that you know about her and Baron. Or just leave your money and property all to her in trust so that slippery, murdering son of a bitch can never get his hands on it."

"I might do just that."

"You won't make me unhappy, Uncle Frank, and you won't make me respect you any less. You've been good to me and good for me, and I appreciate all you've done for me."

"A hell of way you take to show it."

"By wanting to marry your own granddaughter?"

"Don't keep saying that! You don't count relations like that. I *am* going to have a talk with Fanny about Godfrey, and I am going to send word to Foster Bainbridge to come out and talk to me about a new will. If you let me down in these things, you'll let me down in others, too."

"I'm one hundred per cent behind anything you decide to do—except marry me off to Fanny Bannister."

The old man said nothing. His moment of high, hot spirit had died down, and he looked merely old and peevish and helpless. Terence went out into the kitchen and asked Maria to get him off to bed. He slipped on out the back door and headed straight for Eloísa.

Tonight she was sitting primly in a little rocking chair that was her mother's sewing chair in the tiny living room, wearing a floor-length Méxican dress with lots of lace on it. Her hair was quite formally coiled above each ear, and she wore big, circular earrings and carried a lace handkerchief.

She put aside the book she had been pretending to read. "Hello, Terence," she said sedately. "I had about given you up entirely."

He leaned over to kiss her, but she turned her head and gave him her cheek. "No woman likes to be taken for granted," she said. "I think we will behave ourselves tonight."

"I really doubt that," said Terence, who knew her. He knelt on the floor beside the chair. She folded her hands in her lap and looked at him gravely. It was, he knew, just an opportunity to show him another side of her: the way she would look if she ever did become mistress of the Dot M Dot.

CHAPTER 12

On the evening before the sale Sheriff Omar Hall arrived with a big wallet full of shiny new badges. He was a frustrated and somewhat sullen man, angry because the rumors that Baron Godfrey was still in the county were making him look like a fool. He had Terence pick out ten able-bodied, steady, reliable men and deputized them.

"You can always have a rumpus at a big sale, and the best guarantee against it is to have plenty of law in sight," he said. "But all of you know Baron Godfrey, and that's the son of a bitch I'd like to catch sneaking in. Don't try to shoot it out with him unless you've got him outnumbered three to one! Don't be ashamed to holler for help, because that's what I mean to do."

The sheriff ate supper with the family, but Uncle Frank did not. Foster Bainbridge had arrived late in the afternoon with his worn valise of papers and had spent almost all the afternoon with Frank in his room. He did not come down until María brought down their supper dishes, saying the old man was asleep.

It was dark, and the campfires of people who had come a long way to attend the sale twinkled on the hillside east of the house, where there was plenty of forage for teams, water from the windmills, and all outdoors for the kids.

Terence came upon him as he stood in the back yard, puffing on a cigar and thinking. "Hello there, Mr. Bainbridge," Terence said. "Sorry I haven't had a chance to speak to you earlier, but getting ready for a sale is a hell of an organizing job."

"Frank says you're doing an excellent job."

"I'm glad to hear that."

Foster looked down at the ground and scuffed a pattern in the dirt with the toe of his boot. "Terence, mind telling me what has come between you and Frank?"

Terence smiled through the dark. "Mind telling me what makes you think something has?"

"Oh don't be an idiot! I shouldn't have to face that question."

"You mean he's cutting me out of his will."

"You know I can't discuss that."

"You don't have to. He threatened me with it a week and a half ago, and I see no reason to think he has changed his mind."

"Has Fanny Bannister caused you trouble?"

Fanny had avoided him all she could since that last evening at the organ, but they could not avoid meeting in the big house, and she had always been polite if not warmly so.

"There's no trouble she can cause me," he said, "because I don't give a damn. But she can put herself in a bad position and perhaps cause you considerable embarrassment, too."

"How?"

"About Baron Godfrey."

Through the dark, Bainbridge looked surprised. "How did you know about that?"

"She told me. How did you know about it?"

"Frank told me Baron used to have some kind of hold on her, an old affair or something. He's making me conservator and trustee and specifically forbidding me to give her money that I have good reason to believe will go to Godfrey. It can indeed cause me embarrassment."

"You're a good lawyer. Just do your duty, and let nature take its course."

Bainbridge shivered. "And if it brings that back-shooting scoundrel down on me sometime, I can die comforted by knowing that I did my duty. Terence, there's more here than we think, either of us."

"I can't figure it out."

"I tried to talk to Ernest, but he's plainly incompetent, a case of senility. Julia has all her wits and then some, but it's news to her, too, and she knew Fanny in San Francisco and did *not* know Baron Godfrey or anything about him. I wish I could tell you what's in the will we have outlined, but of course I can't."

"Don't let it worry you."

"I've got more bad news for you, too. I'm supposed to get it finished tonight and tomorrow morning so he can sign it, and I've been assigned to your bedroom. You're being evicted doubly."

"I know where I'll sleep."

The lawyer looked at him. "Not, I hope, with Fanny Bannister."

Terence shook his head. "Unless you're too tired, why don't you walk up the slope with me and say hidy to some of tomorrow's bidders? I ought to make myself available if anyone has any questions."

"I can use the walk, but I hope Frank doesn't see us. I tried to talk him out of his folly, and he'll be suspicious that we're conspiring together."

"He's dead to the world until about midnight."

They walked up to where the people were camped. He was known to a few of them and, he thought, better liked than his uncle ever had been. By now he knew most of the good horses that were to be sold tomorrow, too. Horsemanship was more than a business to these people. It was a profession, an art, a way of life, and suddenly to be respected as a horseman himself, a man whose advice and word were good, gave him unexpected stature. He was introduced to many more men and their families before Foster Bainbridge decided he had better get back to the house and begin drafting a new will that would stand up in court.

"This, by the way, is his sixth one," he said as they neared the house. "The more he had to give up management of the ranch, the more interested he became in disposing of it. That comes, I suppose, of having no children of his own."

"He's got a granddaughter."

The lawyer snorted. "I imagine you know how she comes out in—"

Something howled viciously past them, so close that Terence could feel the wind of its passage, and he heard a heavy bullet strike the pepper tree. Both men instinctively threw themselves on the ground, and Terence yanked out his .45. But the long interval between the striking of the bullet and the report of the rifle told him the gunman was too far away for a sidearm.

"Baron Godfrey," Bainbridge whispered. "He's determined to get you one way or another."

They listened for hoofbeats and heard none. One of the Dot M Dot riders who had been deputized came running. The report of the rifle had alarmed him. He collected three other deputies, and they saddled horses and rode up the slope to the camps.

No one had seen the gunman, although several had heard the gun fired from nearby. Godfrey, dismounted, had slipped down and taken cover in a clump of brush and had waited his chance to fire from there. He was long gone by the time they found the spot. He had, beyond doubt, tied his horse farther up the slope and after firing once had beaten a hasty retreat.

With Terence and Bainbridge staying well out of the illuminated area, they lit tinder-dry clumps of brush and found where the man had rolled and smoked five cigarettes as he waited. He had been there at least an hour, since the falling of dark, waiting for a shot. Terence shivered when he thought of how carelessly he had circulated among the campers. Still, it would have been risky shooting with too many witnesses handy, and then Godfrey had not been marksman enough to kill Terence when at last he was in the clear, down near the house.

When he went in, María was just bringing a paper box with his clothing down the stairs. Her dark eyes blazed with anger. "You are out of your room tonight, Terence," she said, "and who knows if you ever get back into it. You come to my house."

Shortly after midnight someone knocked on the door, and he heard a small boy speaking in Spanish. He had just gone to sleep when María tapped softly on the door and came in.

"It is the señor who wants you," she said. "You must come and play the organ for him. He can't sleep."

Terence pulled on his clothes and slipped out quietly. He knew that María would have turned the old ingrate down, but she could get away with it and he could not. A single lamp was burning in the big house, in Uncle Frank's room. He went through the kitchen and climbed the stairs to his own room, opening the door softly.

Foster Bainbridge was sitting at the table in his underwear. He had been writing but had fallen asleep with his head on his arms on the table, which was littered with

sheets of lined foolscap that he had been copying on stiff
white paper.

He went on through into his uncle's room, again closing
the door softly. Frank had sat up on the edge of the bed in
his underwear, his bare feet on the deerskin rug beside his
bed.

"Where the hell you been, boy? I couldn't even raise
María. Lucky thing one of the other women was there to
send for you," he said peevishly.

"I was at María's place."

"Seems to me you're over there too much lately. What if
I need you some night and you're not in your bed and
there's nobody to send for you?"

"Uncle Frank, you gave Foster Bainbridge my room tonight. What do you want me to do, sleep on the floor?"

"Foster Bainbridge? What's he doing here?"

Plainly either the old man was still half asleep, or his
mind was wandering. "You sent for him to draw up a new
will," Terence said patiently.

"Hey? Oh sure, that's right. I forgot. Well, I can't sleep.
Play the organ for me, will you?"

"Uncle, it will wake up everyone in the place. Why not
the violin?"

"No, I bought that organ, and I want to hear it. Find my
dressing robe and slippers, and help me down the stairs. I
ain't going to sleep any more tonight. Tomorrow's the sale,
ain't it?"

"Yes."

"Nobody tells me anything anymore. They think just because I'm ninety-four, I don't know what's going on. Well,
I do, by God! You can't fool me, and neither can anybody
else."

While Terence was helping Frank on with his robe, the

door opened softly and Foster Bainbridge looked in sleepily. Frank kept grumbling. Terence helped him fit his big feet into his slippers and then led him carefully down the stairs, Frank complaining all the way.

"A man works hard all his life, and what does he get out of it? Everybody neglects him when he's old and helpless. Well, by hell, I ain't helpless yet, and I own an organ, and I want to hear it."

They reached the living room. Terence turned Frank's big rocker to face the organ and lighted both lamps over it. He did not feel like playing, but he felt sorry for the old man. The woman who had sent the boy to call him had sent for two to pump the organ.

He sat down and began playing softly, mostly just improvising. Once he looked over and saw Foster Bainbridge standing in his underwear at the foot of the stairs, shaking his head. He looked around at his uncle and saw that he had dozed off. At almost the same moment, Fanny Bannister came down the narrow back stairs, closing her sheer peignoir around her. She had pulled her hair back into tight braids and in this light looked at least forty.

Yet at the same time she had never looked more attractive. She opened her mouth to speak, saw Frank asleep in his chair, and dropped her voice to little more than a whisper.

"What was that you were playing? It was just beautiful, beautiful!" she said.

"Nothing much. Just fooling around with harmonic combinations."

She saw Foster then and gave him a nod and a smile. "Come in and sit down, Foster," she said. "Let's listen to some more of Terence's music."

"I'm hardly dressed for a concert, and I've got work to do."

"Oh I've seen men in their underwear before, and work can always wait. Wasn't it beautiful?"

"It was that, all right. I'll compromise, Fanny. I'll sit here on the stairs, decently concealed, and then go back and get to work."

"I had no idea there was so much folderol to an auction sale that he had to have his lawyer here, too. Poor old man, he's really not very considerate of anyone."

She took a chair close to the organ, and Foster vanished in the stairwell. The two boys began pumping the organ again, and Terence began experimenting with the stops. He found one that had a powerful, flutelike tone and, suppressing its volume, used it to carry most of his melody. His left hand sought out a lively Méxican beat, and he wished that Eloísa could hear it.

Foster stood up after a few moments and waved his thanks before ascending the stairs to work again. Frank slept on. Terence let the voice of the organ die away and signaled to the two boys to stop pumping.

Fanny came over to the console and leaned over Terence, putting her cheek against his.

"Take Uncle Frank back upstairs, and then come to my room," she whispered.

"Now you know I'm not going to do that."

"Not even if I say please?"

"Fanny, you're making as much trouble as you can, aren't you? Did Uncle Frank promise you the money from the sale?"

"No, because you didn't ask him to, did you?"

"Not for that murderer Baron Godfrey."

She gave him a strange look from eyes that burned in a pale face, a look of hopelessness, anger, pitiful appeal—what? With a visible effort she recovered her dignity, turned, and went quietly up the dark stairs at the rear, where she would not encounter Bainbridge. It was impossible not to feel sorry for her.

Terence went over and took his uncle by the elbow. "Uncle Frank, long past bedtime," he said.

The old man awakened with a start. "Hester was just here, wasn't she? Don't lie to me, Hester was here, and you didn't wake me up!"

"There was no Hester here. I don't know of any Hester."

The old man struggled to his feet and, leaning on Terence's arm heavily, allowed himself to be led up the front stairs to his room. Terence got him out of his robe and slippers and into bed.

Frank pointed to the light that gleamed through the door of Terence's room. "Who's in there? Somebody's in your room!"

"Sure, Foster Bainbridge. You've been working his tail off all night."

"Oh. Oh yes, Foster. Let's see, Fanny's here in the house, too, ain't she?"

"Yes. She came down and listened to the organ a minute."

"You played the organ? Why didn't you call me? I like a little pleasure in life, too, goddamn it."

"You called me, Uncle Frank. You were there, but you went to sleep right in the middle of it. Don't you remember?"

"Oh yes, oh yes, I sent Teresa to get somebody to call you. All right, go on back and let me sleep. First give me a glass of rum."

Terence poured him a stiff drink of rum, which the old man shot back with a sigh and a comfortable shudder. He lay down and let Terence cover him and was immediately asleep. When Terence started down the front stairs, he heard his name called softly and turned and saw Foster Bainbridge motioning to him. He went through his own room instead.

Foster closed the door. "This could pose a problem," he said.

"What kind of problem?"

"As foolish and forgetful as he is tonight, I really doubt he's mentally capable of drawing a will. If you and Fanny testify to what you saw and heard, it will probably be thrown out."

"I'll never testify against it. I don't know about Fanny."

Foster grinned his wry grin. "When she sees what's in it, I guarantee she'll defend it to the death."

"I don't want to know any more about it, Foster."

"And you're right. I don't want to talk any more about it, but he had better be sharper tomorrow with all this sale crowd here, I can tell you that. People talk, and if he blathers like that in front of anyone, this could drag on for weeks."

"How much longer will it take you?"

"I've just started the fair copy. He's made it so damned complicated that I'm not going to get done much before noon, and by then you'll have two thousand people on the place."

CHAPTER 13

Terence had planned to get up any time after three in the morning and stir the crew out to get ready for the sale. He was awakened by a big, noisy dogfight, and when he struck a match, his watch showed it was exactly 2:30.

In the *barrio*, dogs had citizenship rights that permitted them to settle their own differences in their own way at any time. But these were big dogs, and he remembered the two belonging to *Pancho de los Leones*. He dressed quickly and went outside. There must have been a hundred dogs on the place, with so many people camped here for the sale, but he easily picked out one of Pancho's dogs. It had whipped another big dog and was standing off two more who were having second thoughts.

He walked up to the dog and snapped his fingers. "*Vaya conmigo*," he said, and the dog went with him, ignoring the threats from other dogs. They circled the house, and the dog led him halfway down to the road to Scobie. There waited Pancho with his other dog.

"Didn't know how else to get hold of you, Terence," he said, "and I've got news for you. I've found where Baron Godfrey is holed up, and I've seen him there twice. He's got a tin can camp down in the tules about five miles to the west. He never has built a fire, near as I can tell. Just lives out of the canned stuff Fanny Bannister brings him."

"Good! Is there any way of surrounding him quickly and taking him before daylight?"

Pancho shook his head. "No cover except the brush he's denned up in, and he's got that forty-four caliber Winchester seventy-three. He don't really sleep. I sneaked up on him once and was a hundred and fifty feet away when he sat up and grabbed for that rifle. I could sic the dogs on him and make a run for him, but he'd get both my dogs and maybe me, too."

"All the same," Terence said, "I don't want him on the loose with this sale crowd around. I'm going to stir Omar Hall and my deputies out and just go after him."

"Get Bill Marquant, too. I seen him here last evening. He's worth a dozen of Omar. I'll wait here and guide you to him."

"Fine. And don't bother to remind me that I guaranteed you a thousand dollars reward. It hasn't slipped my mind, and it won't."

"Never figured it would."

It took half an hour to get the two lawmen and the ten temporary deputies out, mounted, and organized. Most of them already knew Pancho; the others knew of him. They followed him through the dark for several miles. All wore side arms, and there were three Winchesters and two Henry lever-action carbines. And Omar had given orders to shoot to kill.

"He gets one chance to surrender. If he turns it down, pump him full of lead."

Nearing the site of the camp, Pancho stopped and described what lay ahead. They were almost on the hot, rich floor of the valley now, in what practically amounted to a swamp, so high was the ground-water level. Cattle and horses had worn good, solid trails through it. Pancho described them and sent parties of men along each with orders to stop, spread out, and form a picket line and just wait.

Pancho, Terence, Omar, and Bill went straight ahead toward the camp, the dogs almost under their horses' feet. The dark was thinning out as though diluted with water, although the sun had not appeared yet. They rode as quietly as possible, but each squeak of a saddle, each jingle of bit rings made Terence's nerves jump.

Again Pancho reined in. "I'm going to send the dogs ahead to try to spook him out. I hate to risk them, but *ay carrai*, it's better them than us. What if they flush him out?"

"I'll holler for him to surrender, that he's surrounded," said Sheriff Hall. "Unless he comes out with his hands up, pump him full of lead. The others already know. One shot and they cut loose, too."

Pancho spoke to the dogs in Spanish. They ran silently down the trail and vanished into the high tules. Terence felt his heart pound as they waited. "Will they attack if they find him?" he whispered to Pancho.

"Not unless he attacks them. Then the bitch will kill him. She's mean."

Not a sound came from the tules, and in a few minutes the dogs came trotting back. Pancho shook his head and dismounted. "He's not there, but let's make sure. One of you hold my horse, and I'll take a look."

He, too, vanished into the tules, crouching low; he, too, returned immediately. "He didn't spend the night here," he reported. "Come see the way the son of a bitch has been living."

He mounted and led them to a little clearing in the tules. The most distinguishing feature in it was a stack of tin cans. A cheap can opener hung on one of the tules. There were signs where he had spread at least one blanket for a bed, but it was gone. He had a dandy's habit of shaving at least twice a week and trimming his mustache. No sign of the bag that held his razors, strop, hone, and small scissors.

"I got a hunch he's moved on. But where to?" Pancho said.

"And why today, with five or six hundred people camped here for the sale?" said Terence. "Maybe more than that before we get going. Auctioneer says we'll have a thousand, counting families."

Sheriff Omar Hall scratched his jowls and then called for his other men to come in and inspect the camp too. "He's been living like a damned scavenger, and that ain't no vacation. That means it's part of a plan that comes to a head today," he said. "Just in case he does come back, let's kick his pile of cans all the hell over his camp and mess it up for him. But the main thing, we go back and eat in a hurry and start patrolling the sale. And the minute he shows up, cut loose on him before he can kill somebody."

A little disconsolately, they returned to the ranch at a trot.

Pancho promised to prowl the circumference of the sale just in case Godfrey betrayed himself approaching the ranch. "I feel better having him there," said Sheriff Hall, "but I'll still be glad when it's over."

When what was over? Nobody knew. Godfrey's hatred of someone, something, at the Dot M Dot made him an unpredictable, unknown quantity. You could not figure him as you would a normal man, especially when you had no idea what his target was.

The sale lot was a big plank corral adjoining the barb-wire pasture where the horses had been kept. The boys had found a few more up in the hills, horses that had not had human hands laid on them since they were branded as colts and that were wild as deer. It was going to take some handling to cut them out of the herd and get them into the auction pen.

Around the top of the pen planks had been laid to furnish seating for the men who would do the bidding. The auctioneer, Colonel Sawyer, had a little plank platform in a corner of it with a stout railing around it and a desk for his clerk. He was busily getting acquainted with his job when Terence went there to see if there was anything else he needed. Sawyer was a big, pompous man, good at his job, and he had already eaten breakfast. Both Sheriff Hall and Deputy Marquant were eating now; as soon as they came out, their men could eat in the bunkhouse dining room.

Terence saw Hall emerge, wiping his mouth on the back of his hand, and waved to him that he would go eat now himself. He went down to the big house and went in the kitchen door. Eloísa was helping her mother this morning.

"The señor is at the table, wondering where you are," said María. "So are all the others except Señor Bainbridge. He is sleeping yet."

Terence thanked her, washed at the bench outside the kitchen door, and went into the house. His place at Uncle Frank's right hand had been reserved for him. The old man looked rested, bright, and cheerful this morning. He greeted Terence jovially.

"You take your work too damn seriously, boy," he said. "I seen you take a gang out long before daylight. What were you up to?"

Fanny sat at Frank's left, beside Aunt Julia. Next to Julia, Ernest slumped like a massive lump of flesh in which the only proof of life was his shallow breathing. The seat next to Terence had been reserved for Foster Bainbridge.

There was no use lying. He gave Fanny a warning look

and then did not glance at her again. To his uncle he said, "We found where Baron Godfrey has been camped, but he was gone when we got there. He has been holed up there, within five miles of here, for some time. I only wish I knew where is now."

"He better not show his face here," Frank said. "Set down. Julia insists on saying grace, if the rest of us starve to death. Let's get to it."

"Our heavenly Father, we thank Thee for the bounty Thou hast provided. . . ."

On and on she went. Terence dared a glance at Fanny and found her watching him furtively, steadily, although she kept her head bowed. Ernest puttered with his knife, making a tinkling sound on his plate, until Julia put her hand on his to silence it.

The grace ended. María and Eloísa came in bearing big platters of fried beefsteak, fried eggs, and fresh, hot biscuits with beef gravy. Julia rejected all but an egg and a small piece of steak. Fanny filled her plate and ate daintily but hungrily. Ernest merely dawdled with his food, while Frank pitched in with a lusty appetite. Terence found he was hungry, too.

"What's your guess on what we'll net today, Terence?" Frank asked.

"You don't want me to tell you I'm a bad guesser at things like this," said Terence, "so I'll just blunder right in and say about fifty-two hundred."

"About what I figure myself," said Frank. "Some damn good horseflesh there. Horses I'd forgot all about. Just been eating me out of house and home. Ought to round up about a thousand scrub cattle, mostly heifers, and have another sale before cold weather."

"I think that's a good idea."

Frank nodded and cut off a bite of beefsteak and chewed

it strongly. "Nice to have a little ready cash instead of all these damn culls," he said.

Terence caught an appealing glance from Fanny. He felt sorry for her, and he could not help but respond. "Now, that's a lot of nonsense, Uncle Frank," he said. "The last thing in the world you need is ready cash. What would you spend it on?"

"What do you think I should spend it on?"

"Give it to Fanny Bannister. You promised it to her."

"I did like hell!"

"Never mind," Fanny said. "It isn't worth an argument."

"We won't have an argument, Fanny," said Terence, "but I'll say this: If I were ninety-four years old, I'd hate to walk around with a broken promise on my conscience. Uncle Frank, you're a hell of a sport when it comes to talk, but you did get this girl down here on the promise of some money, and now you can't bear to part with it— money you didn't even know you had. What do you want to do, take it with you?"

Frank chuckled. "I ain't ready to go yet. All right, Fanny can have it; I did promise it to her. Only I sure didn't have no idee it would be so much. But the tail goes with the hide, as the feller says."

"You mean that, Uncle Frank?"

Frank gave Terence a mock glare. "By the time you've knowed me sixty or seventy years, you'll know I mean what I say. Soon as the sale is settled up, turn the money over to her. The rest of you are witnesses."

Julia's eyes misted over. "I don't begrudge her a cent of it, but I have to stage a quarrel to get a new dress."

Frank paid no attention to her. Frank pointed his knife at Fanny. "One thing, though," he said. "Not a goddamn cent goes to Baron Godfrey."

Fanny shook her head and began crying softly. "That's a promise, Uncle Frank," she said. "If it's that much, I'll be free of him forever."

Terence did not understand her, and this was not the time to ask. They finished the meal, and he went up to the auction pen, where the first worthless colt had just been brought in for bidding. Julia, who had never seen a ranch horse auction, went with him, clinging to his arm. Behind them, Ernest had taken his usual place on the bench under the pepper tree, oblivious to the excitement farther up the slope.

Colonel Sawyer was doing his best to get the bidding started. "All right, five dollars. Four! Say, listen, I'm not going any lower than that for a filly coming on two. Anybody here want a *free* horse?"

A moment of silence. Then a teen-age boy piped up, "I do!"

"Sold to the Goldring kid for zero dollars. Get a rope on her, son, and get her the hell out of here so we can get some horses in here."

Willing hands helped rope the horse and secured her with a strong halter. The Goldrings obviously were poor people; even a worthless horse was important to them. The whole family helped the boy lead his young mare down and tie her firmly to the wheel of their wagon.

The next horse was a hammerheaded gelding of about four. He would be hard to break, but he had the look of strength and speed, and the bidding was brisk before he went for eighty-five dollars. The next, a wild but handsome brood mare heavy with foal went for an even hundred.

"I'm afraid I'm not going to be able to stand much more, Terence," Julia quavered. "It's so loud and dusty and tiring. Will you take me back to the house?"

"Of course, Aunt Julia. But it's something you should see, isn't it?"

"Very well, I've seen it. How are the prices running? What do you think it will bring in?"

"Probably a little more than I estimated, but at least that much."

"I'm glad for Fanny's sake. I owe her nothing, in fact I dislike her intensely, but she has had a hard time of it."

"In what way?"

They were walking slowly down the slope in the hot sun, she leaning heavily on his arm. "Don't you know? Mr. Bannister was a thorough gentleman and a money-maker. Had he lived, she would have been able to live like the lady she really is, but he died just as the business got on its feet. And then that *damned* Baron Godfrey began courting her and got it all. Forty thousand dollars!"

"How in the world did a man like him get to know her?"

She said wearily, "It's ancient history, and I suppose you can be forgiven for not knowing. Mr. Bannister was financed by Frank. They were good friends. Frank was uncharacteristically generous in allowing her to settle the estate on the most favorable terms. She had the greatest respect for him, and he deserved it in this case at least. Not like the Viscainos at all."

"Had an eye on her himself, maybe?"

"Not at all. He was far too old for that. It was just one of the unexpected things he's always doing. Baron came to her and told her he was Frank's illegitimate son and asked her help in getting an introduction to Frank."

"Surely that's fiction."

"Nothing else! Frank hired a detective to run down his

background. His parents were both living in Frankfort, Kentucky. He was two years in the Kentucky penitentiary for fraud. The man's not even a smart crook."

She had tired badly by the time they reached the kitchen. He had become very fond of her in the last few weeks, dating, he supposed, back to the time when Ernest lost his power to promote trouble and ill feeling. He helped her into the kitchen and started through to take her up the stairs.

"Better go see about the señor," María said. "He is asleep in his rocker on the front porch. Once he went to sleep and slipped down and hurt his head. I can do nothing with him."

A glance through the open door showed Frank tilted dangerously forward. "Sit down and wait here, Aunt Julia," Terence said. "María, better give me a hand, please."

María dried her hands on her apron. "Not ten minutes past he went out, and look how deeply he sleeps!" she said. "Ay carrai, how easily he could fall. We must take him up for his nap."

"He doesn't look right," Julia said. "Let me come, too."

Terence opened the door but did not let the women precede him. Just as he stepped out onto the porch, Frank McNeil started to pitch forward, off balance. Terence let go of the screen and jumped to catch him and pull him back.

One look at his gray, slack face told him the truth. He did not need to see the great gouts of blood that had spouted from the old chest and were congealing on his body.

"Jesucristo, es muerte!" María moaned, crossing herself.

Eloísa appeared in the living room, just behind the screen. Terence said, "Go wake Foster Bainbridge and tell him Uncle Frank has been killed. Send somebody up to

find Omar Hall or Bill Marquant, and tell them to keep
that damned crowd away from the house. And ask them to
ask around and try to find out if anybody heard a shot."

You did not have to repeat instructions to Eloísa. She
vanished. "Shot?" Julia said faintly. "Who would shoot a
ninety-four-year-old man?"

"You know who!" he said savagely. "Shot with a forty-
four caliber rifle from quite a way off. Look, who could get
close enough to shoot him with a forty-five? Besides, someone in the house would have heard it. Somebody stood
down there—or knelt down there or shot from prone position—and centered on his heart. And only a few minutes
ago. My God, he's still warm to the touch!"

CHAPTER 14

His first thought had to be of Aunt Julia, but she stood it better than he had any reason to hope she would. It was Fanny Bannister who went to pieces, who aged thirty years in as many seconds, whose mind refused to believe the only truth that counted: that Frank McNeil was dead.

The auctioneer behaved magnificently. Omar Hall got him aside for a whispered explanation. Colonel Sawyer went to the edge of his platform, held up his hands for attention, and announced that Frank McNeil had been murdered by gunfire on his own front porch.

"We're pretty sure Baron Godfrey did it, but that's the sheriff's business. I'm going to go ahead with this sale because it's the last thing I can do for Frank. I hope you'll put it out of your minds and help make this last sale a success, and *stay away from that house!* Leave them to their sorrow, and let us get on with our business."

Omar Hall staked all on his theory that Godfrey would circle the house, head for the hill to the east, and strike out for the wilds of the Sierra Nevada. There was no place in the Central Valley he could hide, with Wanted posters already up everywhere and citizens as well as peace officers looking for him. Hall would take six well-mounted and well-armed men and head for the northeast and an old cattle trail that had been cut off years ago by Frank's fences. Bill Marquant would strike south and then turn east, where the foothills ran a little farther before the steep elevations began. Frank had kept four binoculars in the house; Terence was able to give one to each posse.

As for himself, he knew that *Pancho de los Leones* wanted to talk to him privately, and he waited for a chance while helping fit out the two posses. The two men met in the dark corner of the big haybarn, from where they could hear the mesmeric chant of Colonel Sawyer. It seemed to Terence that people were bidding more recklessly than they had been. Why?

Frank McNeil had few friends around here and many enemies. There was no sentiment in these bids. No, it seemed to him that the basic reason they were going so high was that this was their last chance to skin Frank in a deal. It was almost a certainty that no more big auctions would be held here, and they had better make this one pay off.

"You and me," said Pancho, "I think we should go for a certain place I know, on fresh horses. His will be tired. You know that cutting and branding pen up above the creek yonder?"

"Yes, of course, but that's four or five miles away."

"Yes, he hasn't had time to get there yet. Go past it to a stand of timber that looks like you're shut off by a high climb. That ain't so. That's where the deer come down in the fall and go back again in the spring. I don't think many people know about it, but the pumas do, and I do. It would give this bastard a head start we could never catch him, *sabe?*"

"If he knows about it."

"He must. He may be a madman, but he's not a fool. He would have an escape route picked out, and there is no other. Give us big, strong horses and plenty of ammunition for forty-fives, a Winchester, and a Henry. Because somewhere on that trail is where we'll find him."

"All right, I'll go get the ammunition and a bait of trail grub, but no shooting when we sight him. This bastard comes back to hang."

"If we can. He will know there is no ending possible but the rope if he comes back. He may as well shoot it out."

"If he feels that way, let me shoot it out with him, not you."

He chose two powerful horses, both stallions, and told Pancho to start saddling them. He hurried to the house to load up with ammunition and to ask María to prepare food for the trail. He asked where Eloísa was.

"In the house, praying," the *llavera* said gently. "He was her grandfather, after all. Go say good-by, even if only for a minute."

He shouldered the flour sack of food and ammunition and went around to the little house where María and Eloísa lived. He knocked gently and identified himself but got no answer. He opened Eloísa's private door into her bedroom and went through it into the little living room.

In a corner of it hung a shrine to the Virgin, to which he had never paid much attention except to be aware that there was always a candle lighted before it. The girl he loved—and he had never loved her more than now—knelt on a cushion before it. She did not even hear him until he came up and put his hand on her shoulder.

"Eloísa!"

She looked up, startled out of a religious passion so deep that it had contained only herself and the Mother of God. He lifted her to her feet and let her put her arms around him and just hang on while, gently, he kissed her cheeks and temples and hair.

"I loved him; I truly did," she said. "He was my *viejo*, and he never said a bad thing to me in all my life."

"I know," he said. "I fought with him because I had to.

My job was different than yours, but I loved the old hellion in my own way."

She stroked his cheek. "I know you did or you would not have stayed here. Oh my beloved man, what happens now?"

"I don't know. The first thing we've got to do is bring in Baron Godfrey."

"And give the señor burial on his own place. Years ago he picked out a spot for his grave. *Mi mamá* knows where it is. Can I tell her that will be the place?"

"Of course. She's in charge until I get back."

"God be praised for your understanding heart."

He stroked her hair and gazed at her lovely, tawny face. So meek and yet so dignified, so helpless and yet so strong. They kissed once, without passion, and she turned her back to kneel on her cushion and resume her prayers for her old hellion of a grandfather who now would never reach one hundred years of age.

Uneasy about the crowd of roughnecks that always attended auction sales, he locked the door carefully behind him as he went out. He saw María coming toward him.

"Don't worry; no one will bother her," she said. She took a small pistol from her apron pocket. "I have not carried this in many, many years, but the señor himself taught me to shoot it, and I have not forgotten."

He leaned over to kiss her cheek. "*Mamacita*," he murmured, and she pulled his head down to kiss his own cheek before returning to the house.

Behind the house, near the pepper tree, a fire was burning, attended by Uncle Ernest. He was squatting and feeding sheets of paper into it one at a time. Foster Bainbridge came out with another handful of papers, squatted down, and began to burn them, too.

"What's all this?" Terence asked.

"I don't know what Ernest is burning," said Foster. "Ask him."

"My diary for thirty years. Oh I never kept it regularly! Whole months went by without a word. But I often had great anger against my brother, and I don't want that record to survive."

He seemed, in the way of the senile, to have momentarily recovered command of himself. He had shaved and changed his shirt and altogether had tidied himself as best he could at his age and in his physical condition. He gave Terence a bitter smile and said, "You are his blood kin, too. It would be more becoming if you dressed to show respect."

"Nothing would be more becoming than for me to help run down the son of a bitch that killed him."

"Baron?"

"Yes."

Ernest slid off into his world of reverie without a sign of acknowledgment. Foster Bainbridge held up the bundle of papers he was feeding into the fire. "His new will. I never even got a chance to finish drawing it. Now the old one will stand unrevoked," he said.

"When will we hear it read?"

"When you have come back from trying to catch Baron Godfrey, which I don't think you can do. Don't stay out overnight. Come back, all of you, and get a good night's sleep so we can hold the funeral tomorrow, and then I'll read the will. I'll have to go get it, and while I'm at it, I'll get Father Truxton to come up and read the services."

"Father Truxton?"

"He's an old man, too, in his eighties. Father Pohl would have nothing to do with it, even though Frank was born a Catholic."

"The hell you say! I know my mother was a fallaway

Catholic, but I never knew it was in this side of the family, too."

"The reason she could not live her faith was that she divorced another man to marry your father, and so they both lived in a state of sin. Father Truxton will find some judicial chute through which he can herd a requiem mass, even if it's by a split decision. Father Pohl will be furious, and the bishop will scold Father Truxton, but when you get to a certain age, those things don't matter so much anymore."

"What about Uncle Ernest and Aunt Julia?"

"Julia married out of the church. It wasn't quite fashionable in parts of California. The war against México was in a sense a religious war, and you could count on the McNeils being on the winning side. Ernest never married."

"I see." Terence swung his bag up over his shoulder again.

"You had better do a lot of thinking. You are going to be in a position of great responsibility and will have some big decisions to make under the old will."

"We'll see."

"You can't just slide out from under, Terence. You've got to play the hand that's dealt you."

"We'll see," Terence said again. He circled the sale pen to the barn, where *Pancho de los Leones* was having his problems keeping two aggressive stallions from attacking each other. They found a gunny sack and divided the trail rations and ammunition into two saddle packs. They mounted and, with Pancho in the lead, set off up the slope between the live oaks. At the first gate, two hours away, Terence dismounted to open it, but Pancho said, "Stop! First let me see if there is anything to see here."

He got off his horse and came to the gate, handing his reins to Terence. The gate was composed of four wires strung between two stout poles. At one end there was a loop of wire into which one of the poles was set. The top was secured by a hardwood pry bar that kept the wires of the gate taut and that was held by a ring of wire which simply slipped over it.

"I knew I was right," Pancho said with satisfaction. "He opened this gate, too. He held it and led his horse through, and here's the hoof that's badly shod. *Caramba!* He must think we're idiots."

They closed the gate and waited while the two big dogs sniffed around at the tracks. The bad-tempered bitch seemed to get the idea. She put her nose to the ground and went loping easily up the slope. The other dog followed. Not once did they show doubt as to where they were going; not once did Pancho lose faith in them. "They'll save us a lot of time," he said. "We won't have to look for tracks. They'll know!"

About three hours later Pancho called the dogs back and put them on leashes. He said nothing, but it was clear he felt they were getting too close. The grade was getting steeper, and the dogs had been following a trail that took advantage of every shallowly slanting canyon.

Periodically, Pancho dismounted to study the trail where it was clearest. He did not have to speak. His look of satisfaction told Terence that they were gaining rapidly on Godfrey now. The fugitive's horse was tiring.

Terence did not know how far eastward the Dot M Dot range extended, and Pancho was not sure. Certainly by the time they reached the tall timber, they were off McNeil land. A little to the north, Pancho said, were logging camps, but Godfrey would avoid them and the roads between them. Almost straight east was the south edge of the

Mother Lode country, where a man could run into a gold seeker at any moment. There were probably thousands who had not yet given up the search for gold in the mountains just above them.

Late in the afternoon Pancho stopped suddenly. The horses had been scrambling up a steep slope of bare, decomposed granite in which the trail of Godfrey's horse was clear. Too clear, it seemed to Terence. Surely less than an hour had passed since that track was made, perhaps only a matter of minutes. The dogs were straining at their leashes, and the bad-tempered female was whining eagerly. Pancho got down and led his horse and the dogs up the sliding slope to where the sparse, dry grass led in among the pines. Terence followed.

"I think," Pancho said slowly, "that we had better separate here. Let me take the dogs and follow with the carbine. You leave the trail and push your horse hard and try to get around him with the Winchester. We're too close for safety if he's got a Winchester, too."

Terence shook his head. "No, I'll stay with the trail. I want to take him alive, and I don't want any rifle duels."

"I wasn't thinking of that. I was thinking that if we shot his horse and put him afoot, it would change everything."

"How do you plan to do that?"

"Hike on as fast as I can and watch his tracks. When I think I'm getting close enough, turn the dogs loose and run after them. I'll fire one shot for a signal to you. If he shoots one of my dogs, you'll know which way to go to find him."

Terence thought it over. "I think we ought to stay together awhile yet. I don't think we're that close."

Pancho closed his eyes to think it over. He opened them. "Another idea. Fire a shot with the Winchester to let him know we're on his tail and hurry him a little. His horse can't stand hurrying. Maybe he'll go lame; maybe he'll cast a shoe. Who knows?"

"That makes sense, but let's get a little farther up in the pines before we do it."

Pancho nodded and remounted. The bitch leaned on the leash, and Pancho had to take a half hitch around his saddle horn to hold her. Half an hour later he stopped, shaking his head.

"Now," he said. "He is too close already. I feel it."

"All right, I'll feel it, too, then," Terence said with a grin. He dismounted and unstrapped the big Winchester, handing the reins of his stud to Pancho. He walked ahead through the trees, Pancho following with the two dogs and the two horses.

He came to an open glade no more than two hundred feet across and stopped. There were fresh droppings here and sign that Godfrey had stopped to feed and rest his horse. Terence went around the open glade and entered the trees again.

Suddenly he heard it, the panting of a tired, overworked horse coming at a trot down the slope. He looked around at Pancho to see if he had heard it, too. The old lion hunter stood up, nodding and squinting.

In a moment a riderless horse appeared among the trees. It was a horse familiar to Terence because it had stood in Dot M Dot corrals for almost a year, part of Baron Godfrey's saddle string, his own horse. It was favoring one hind foot slightly as it headed with some determination for the only home it knew.

It saw the two stallions and threw up its head and stopped. Then it broke into a limping trot to circle them. Pancho made no move to catch it. He hurried with the dogs and the horses to catch up with Terence.

"Notice anything about him?" he asked.

"Two things," said Terence. "He lost a hind shoe, and the Winchester isn't on him. So he didn't throw Godfrey. Godfrey got off and turned him loose to ambush us on foot."

"Yes. We wanted him afoot, and now we have him, but he could be twice as dangerous."

"I know that, but we're still going to take him alive. So if it comes to a shoot-out, go for his legs and arms, not his body."

"It can be done. I don't think he has the patience this job takes. What would our horses do if we turned them loose, too?"

"Head for home as hard as they could hell it."

"Terence, they are just a nuisance now. We can hide our grub and go after him on foot. Never fear, the dogs will find him now." He pointed to the bitch. "She knows! She will make the difference."

They removed their packs and hid them in the brush. They pulled off saddles and bridles and whacked the two stallions across their rumps and sent them galloping back down the slope. All three horses would have to stop at the fence when they got there, with no one to open the gate, but that was a long way away.

They separated, Terence climbing the canyon wall to get a little ahead of Pancho. Pancho waited until he had done so before letting the dogs lead him up the gentler slope of the canyon floor. He had tied the leashes together and held them in his left hand, with the Henry carbine, cocked and with a bullet in the chamber, held like a pistol in his right.

On they climbed, every sound they made magnified by the stillness of the forest. The bitch dug into the dirt with her claws, whining with a sound that meant she knew she was close to her prey.

Terence saw Pancho go down, heard the thud of the slug and then the bellow of the Winchester. Hit high in the shoulder near the neck, Pancho let go of the dogs and tried to roll to cover in the brush. Another slug buried itself in the dirt within inches of him.

And this one gave Terence the sight of Godfrey that he needed. The ragged, unkempt man had leaned over a rock about four feet high to steady his gun to take his shots. Terence dropped to his knee and leveled the Winchester. The dogs raced silently up the canyon toward Godfrey, and Godfrey turned the gun to draw a bead on them.

It turned him half sidewise and gave Terence his target, a shoulder. He squeezed one off and felt the satisfying thud of the gun against his own shoulder and the keen pleasure a man always felt the moment he fired and knew he had hit his mark.

Godfrey screamed and tumbled backward, but he came up on one knee with his left arm hanging uselessly, the Winchester clutched back against his right shoulder. He saw Terence and fired once, and Terence knew the slug had missed him by five or six feet.

"Drop the gun, Baron," he shouted. "You're under arrest, and you're only making it worse on yourself because you're not getting away from us."

Baron rested the gun across the rock. Terence could hear him groan with the agony of the effort. Terence stepped behind a tree, and just then the dogs were on Godfrey. He screamed and went over backward, the gun going off straight up into the air.

Terence left his shelter and sprinted recklessly down the slope. Baron kept screaming. He was out of sight now, somewhere behind the rock. Terence leaped up on top of the rock with the Winchester aimed down at the ground.

Godfrey had dropped his gun and was trying to protect

his throat from the slavering bitch. Terence jumped for the leash, caught it, pulled her off. He leaned his own Winchester against the rock and leveled his .45 at Godfrey. He put his foot on Godfrey's Winchester, the one that used to hang in the kitchen behind the door.

"This is all the chance you get," he said. "I want that forty-five, too. Either hand it over carefully, carefully, or I turn her loose on you again."

Godfrey had lived too long on short rations, hatred, defeat, and desperation. He was hard to recognize as the sport with the waxed mustaches who had been so offended by the handcuffs when he had to stand for a coroner's jury. He made no effort to resist when Terence leaned over to take his .45. He was a thin, bearded, haunted caricature of the man he had once been, and now he could look forward to another trial and then hanging.

Terence left the dogs to guard him and went down to see about Pancho, who was up on his knees, trying to examine his own wound. "It hurts like hell," he said, "but he didn't hit any bone. Make me a bandage and a sling from the flour sack and your handkerchief, and let's start back downhill."

"Are you sure you're in any shape to walk?"

Pancho de los Leones gave him a contemptuous look. "I show you my back where an old she-lion rip the hell out of it while I'm lay on my belly and let her to keep her from my throat. Doctor, he took ninety stitches. You think this is bad?"

Baron's wound was worse. Terence's slug had hit him in the arm about an inch below the shoulder joint, shattering it. If he lived to hang, it would be as a one-armed man.

They were half an hour getting the two wounded men ready for the trail, and by then Omar Hall and his crew had come up, leading the two studhorses that Terence and

Pancho had ridden. They had heard the shooting, recognized the sound of Winchesters, and known instantly what it meant.

The two wounded men were put on gentle horses. One horse had to carry double even after they caught Godfrey's lame horse.

"I have to warn you that anything you say will be used against you," Hall said, "but one thing sure puzzles me: Why the hell did you kill that old man? That seemed like a plain senseless thing to do."

Godfrey looked too weak to talk, but he got it out somehow. "The old son of a bitch ran everything, everybody. Lie, steal, fornicate and get away with it. Well, he won't no more! I turned out to be the best man, finely, didn't I?"

"That's no answer."

"It's all you're going to get."

Terence said, "You think this is going to do you any good with Fanny Bannister? You killed Frank before he had a chance to sign his new will, before Foster even had a chance to finish it. The old one will be the last will and testament of Frank McNeil. Make you feel any better?"

Godfrey swayed in the saddle and went pallid. A deputy had to reach out and catch him to keep him from falling to the ground. He did not speak another word all the way back to the ranch.

CHAPTER 15

Father Truxton was a massive man, dignified and intelligent. Father Pohl drove him up from Santa Margarita's in a buggy, showing none of the disapproval he surely felt. The grave had been dug on a little hillock a few hundred yards from the house. Three live oak trees grew on it, and Frank's plans had included a stone fence around it, some irrigation canals, and rows of Lombardy poplars.

More than three hundred people surprised Terence by turning out for the rites. Benches were brought from the bunkhouse for the family. Aunt Julia was perfectly composed; she had got over the shock of murder, and death was a mere incident at her age. Uncle Ernest was still in one of his elevated moods, and he kept his silence and comported himself with dignity.

Behind them sat Terence with Eloísa and María. Terence did not know the mass well enough to see what Father Truxton left out to appease Father Pohl. The whole crowd waited for the grave to be filled in and mounded. Later, Father Truxton announced, a granite column twenty inches square and ten feet long would be set deeply at the head of the grave, only half of it above ground. It would have a chip finish except for a polished plaque on which a Merced stonecutter was already carving the words

FRANCIS XAVIER McNEIL
August 1, 1794
October 22, 1888

None of the Viscainos attended, but Ed Mitchell did, and so did an entire Méxican family by the name of Martínez. They had once owned the eight-thousand-acre Possum Track tract before Barr and Robertson had cheated them out of it. Vicente Martínez asked Foster Bainbridge for permission to camp on the Dot M Dot tonight and tomorrow to take his numerous family to see the land he had once owned forty years ago.

"Sí, seguro," said Foster, and then called the McNeil family into the house for the reading of the will. There was no question but what it would stand up in court, he said. "I am not responsible for the contents, the meaning, of it. I was instructed to draw a will that would survive any assault in the courts, and this I am sure I have done."

He cleared his throat and began reading. A trust fund of two hundred thousand dollars had already been set up in a San Francisco bank. The moment the will cleared probate, payment of ten thousand dollars was to be made to his sister, Julia, in her own right and a like amount to her as fiduciary guardian of their brother, Ernest.

In addition, quarterly payments of three hundred dollars were to be made to Julia, Ernest, Fanny Bannister, María González de Sánchez, and Eloísa Sánchez González. None of the women was to receive a cent in cash.

Terence, sitting between María and Eloísa, patted María's hand.

"I never expected a cent," she whispered.

Julia, Ernest, María, and Eloísa all had the right to remain on the Dot M Dot as residents, not guests, without the payment of money, so long as they lived.

The balance of the estate, including what remained of the trust after its last beneficiary had died, went to Terence. The old man had insisted that one last word of caution be added:

And I warn him that property is not accumulated by acts of foolish charity. He is very young and impulsive, and while I do not limit him in his possessory rights, I urge him to remember how long and hard I worked to earn all this money and land and livestock.

Fanny looked bewildered, broken, and unable to comprehend what had happened. Ernest had slid gently back into his warm nest of nonunderstanding.

Julia was in full possession of her faculties. She turned to put her hand on Terence's shoulder. "He sounds like a mean old man," she whispered, "but in his way he was right. This whole state was stolen, and he stole only a few thousand acres under laws that would not stand up now. Well, they did then. He was a man of his times."

"I'm going to consult Foster about being a man of my times, Aunt Julia," Terence whispered back. "Will you do something for me? Ask the two priests to spend the night here if possible. At least the afternoon. I want to talk to them."

"I'm sure they expect to be asked."

"First, though, I want to talk to Fanny as soon as Foster is through."

Foster was saying, "I think the appraiser will turn in an appraisal of about one million two hundred thousand dollars—plus, of course, the trust that is already in existence. Terence and I will have to go to San Francisco soon so he can see just what his uncle left him in the way of real property. Some pieces he bought for a few hundred dollars each are now worth forty and fifty thousand each. So, Terence, I hope you will hold yourself in readiness to go up there with me one of these days."

"Of course." Terence leaned over to whisper to Eloísa. "I've got to talk to Fanny quickly, before she breaks down. Help me get her aside into a room somewhere."

María stood up. "Let me. It is too much to ask of a girl who has just been insulted by the grandfather she loved."

"I can agree with that."

As the meeting broke up, Terence and María got Fanny between them and led her, half dazed, into a quiet corner of the living room. She had to be helped to sit down, and then María sat close to her, stroking her wrists.

"Fanny," said Terence, "I just want you to understand that this will means nothing where you're concerned. He owed you a lot more than that, and he promised you a lot more, and you're going to get still more."

There was a perceptible pause before she could marshal her thoughts to say, "I'll believe that when I see it."

"You'll see it. You want to go back to San Francisco to live, don't you?"

"Not on any one hundred dollars a month."

"I want to buy you a house, settle some money on you that will yield a decent income, three or four hundred a month besides what you get from the trust. But until the court frees the money, I want you to stay here and rest and get your soul back."

"I never had one," she said.

"I think now we're getting to what I want to know. Why was Uncle Frank so interested in you, and what was the connection with Baron Godfrey? And if you would rather tell me in complete confidence, María won't mind leaving us alone."

María stood up. Fanny shook her head. "No, I don't care now who knows it. Frank found me when I was just sixteen. I'd been working in a whorehouse for almost a year. No, he didn't want me for himself; he just had one of those fits where he was going to square things for somebody, and this time it was me.

"He took me to friends of his to live with and had them help me buy appropriate clothing. He introduced me to my husband, the finest man that ever lived. He lent us the money to start the tannery in San Mateo. He was like a father to me, never like a lover. Even after my husband's death, when I was foolishly squandering the estate, he used to send me money when I ran short. He was just—kind."

"Kind enough to pick me out as a second husband for you?"

She nodded. "He knew what I was, but he said I would be the proper *patróna* to keep the house here. He warned me about Eloísa, and said there would be others. And, Terence, I truly would have lived up to the deal. I understand such things, and he made it clear, you know, about the *patrón* and his *casitas* and families of children from which to pick an heir."

"One more painful thing. Your husband was murdered, wasn't he?"

"Stabbed for a little more than a thousand dollars he had on him."

"Did you know Baron Godfrey then?"

"He worked for us."

"Were you having an affair with him?"

"No, but the temptation was there. I never fooled around with him while my husband was alive, but we became lovers soon after that."

He looked her straight in the eye for a long time before saying, "Fanny, how long have you been convinced that Baron murdered your husband, too?"

"I've faced that question long enough not to be afraid of it," she said steadily. "I believe I should have known from the beginning, but I was young and stupid and passionately attached to him. It took me a long time to realize how degrading our relationship was. I think it was about then that it suddenly came over me that he had killed Louis. I have never had a moment's peace of mind since, and when I heard he had hired out here and attached himself to Ernest—" She shuddered and choked up.

He nodded to María to take her to her room and make her comfortable. "It's all behind you now, Fanny," he said. "It will take you a little time to believe that, but it's the truth. Uncle Frank only half paid his debt to you. I think if he had only listened, if he had shown any good sense at all, Baron would have been run out of here and he would be alive today."

Wes Peterson, he of the broken leg, came hobbling on his crutch to say that the two priests were waiting in the bunkhouse any time he wanted to see them. Terence thanked him and went to where the two men sat in cowhide easy chairs in the big, empty room. It was beginning to get cold, and he stopped first to stoke the stove before joining them.

"Thank you for waiting," he said, "I'm sure you know what I want to talk to you about."

Father Pohl deferred to the older man. "I think so," said Father Truxton, "but I should like to hear you state it in your own terms."

"I want to marry Eloísa Sánchez as soon as I can. I want her in this house, running it as its mistress. I don't want any other women, no *casitas*, no degrading harems. I was baptized a Catholic and started to learn my catechism, but that stopped when I was about seven, when my mother became angry because the priest would not let her attend mass. If there is no other way out, I will convert, but I would rather just marry and let her raise the children in her own faith."

"My, my!" said Father Truxton. "You'd strike a hard bargain with the Mother Church, wouldn't you?"

"It has struck a hard bargain with me and mine all these years."

Father Truxton glanced at his junior. "Father, we shall have to find a way to Christianize this family. I imagine it will be a big one before they're through, and it pleases me to see a Mexican woman elevated to the status she deserves."

Father Pohl said nothing, but Terence stopped worrying. He felt sure that the bishop would receive a visit from Father Truxton soon and that something would be worked out. *Unión libre* was all very well with the swarms of poor, but it could not be tolerated among the McNeils.

Terence received a statement from Foster saying that more than thirty thousand dollars was available to pay the "just bills" of the decedent but that it would be a matter of taking up each of Terence's proposals in order when it came to probate. The thirty thousand dollars might as well have been thirty dollars.

Three weeks and five conferences with the priests passed before he was given permission to marry Eloísa. He had to agree to raise their children in the faith, see to it that they learned their catechism, and in effect maintain a Catholic household whether he ever became a Catholic himself or not. A nuptial high mass was announced for the week following, and that night he sent word to Angelo and Patricio Viscaino that he wanted to see them.

Back came word that they did not want to see him. He

sent the messenger, Shorty Gubbison, straight back with a request that they meet at the gate between the so-called Viscaino tract and the rest of the Dot M Dot. When he arrived, the two scowling, black-bearded young men were waiting on the other side of the fence. He did not dismount, and they did not open the gate.

"I want to square what my uncle did to your family, and that is my only purpose in meeting with you," he said.

"Give us back our father and our brother. How can you square things without doing that?"

"I am not to blame for that, and neither was Uncle Frank. They were killed by the same murderer who killed Uncle Frank, and we spared no effort to put him where he is. If you want to put a cash value on the deaths of Pete and Marco, that's something new to me."

Neither man answered. He gave them a chance to think it over and then went on. "You came here to raise black muscat grapes and sheep. You paid thirty-five hundred dollars for this land. You borrowed twelve thousand from Uncle Frank and then another two thousand to fence it and import your muscat seedlings. He was not to blame and I am not to blame that they all died on the ship coming over.

"Nevertheless seedlings are now available. So are sheep. The property is fenced. I'm delayed by the court in settling the will, but I have already notified the judge that I mean to return the property to your mother and to pay her fifteen thousand dollars in damages.

"I've got to settle with Ed Mitchell and the Martínez family yet, and I don't need to tell you what trouble it would cause if it got out that I offered the Viscainos that kind of settlement. They're just not entitled to as much, and they can sue if they think they are. But I would like to have a handshake agreement that you and I can settle this way before I go on my honeymoon because when I get back, I imagine we'll be able to close out this case."

They could not believe him. "The property back and fifteen thousand in cash?" Angelo said in a strangled voice.

"Yes."

They looked at each other, and then Angelo met Terence's eyes. "I never expected to see the day when a McNeil would give up something he had his hands on. No catch to it?"

"Yes, I want you two to be responsible for running the Dot M Dot while I'm gone. Foster Bainbridge will keep you informed on the progress of the court case. He agrees that it's a fair settlement that your father would have approved."

"Shake!"

First Angelo and then Patricio put his hand across the fence. Peace between these bitter men and the heir of Frank McNeil was hard to believe after all these years, but it had come at last, and now they could hardly wait to get home to tell their mother.

Negotiations with Ed Mitchell were unfriendly and were made more so by the slowness of the court. There was no way Terence could hand over sufficient money to satisfy a hardfisted man who wanted his land back and who was not entitled to it legally or morally. It was not until the afternoon before the wedding that they all signed a memorandum agreement prepared by Foster Bainbridge under which Terence would pay Mitchell forty-five hundred dollars as soon as the money became his.

The Martínez claimants by now numbered 105. A lawyer patiently listed all of them and their relationship to the original Martínez brothers, but a schedule of indemnities ranging from one thousand dollars each to one hundred dollars each, a total of eighty-three hundred dollars, was at last reduced to a memorandum and signed.

There were other claimants that Terence ignored. Frank McNeil had gone out of his way to antagonize people, and the rumor that Terence was paying off old enemies in cash spread fast and wide. Perhaps a few of them had been cheated out of a few dollars by Uncle Frank; if so, it had happened when they were trying to cheat him, too. That was how business was done in the old days.

"I am not going to undo everything Uncle Frank did," Terence told Foster. "I'll correct the worst injustices, the ones that had meanness and spite in them, but I won't make him a thief in cases where he wasn't one. And the quicker that gets around, the happier I'll be."

He knelt at last before the altar with Eloísa to be made man and wife. Most of the ritual came back to him dimly from his earliest childhood, when his mother had tried to bring him up in her old faith. He slipped the ring on Eloísa's finger, and then Father Pohl took each by an elbow and raised them to their feet for the bridal kiss.

It was a splendid and holy moment to take her in his arms publicly and then take her back to the house as his wife. They would use his old room until they got back from the honeymoon in San Francisco. By then María would have changed everything in Uncle Frank's big bedroom so that they could sleep there without a single reminder of the past.

For the time being, Fanny, Aunt Julia, and Uncle Ernest would retain their bedrooms, and María would remain as *llavera*—more than housekeeper, let it be understood.

"What about when we come back?" Terence asked his bride.

"Oh Mamá will go on being *la llavera*. I will be *la señora*. But leave it to us; we know how these things are done," said Eloísa.

I'll bet you do, he thought.

CHAPTER 16

Eloísa had never been farther from the Dot M Dot than Merced, but they were in San Francisco for three weeks. He bought her clothes she never would need on the ranch but in which she could appear in the best places in the city. She had a sweet serenity that was new to her. It made her prettier than ever and love-making more of an adventure.

They returned after Foster notified them by mail that the judge had closed probate proceedings, and he was free to proceed as he had planned. Angelo and Patricio had run a taut ship in his absence, and the hands were glad to see him back.

"I forgot what color the goddamn house was painted because I never saw it by daylight," Shorty Gubbison complained. "He had us in the saddle before the sun came up, and now he's got the guts to want some of us to work for them in their goddamn vineyards."

"Are you going?"

"Hell, no—none of us! We're cattlemen, not farmers. He's going to bring over a lot of goddamn relatives from Portugal. Listen, I was past one of them wineries down by San Bernardino once. There's people like the smell of them, but not me. Do you realize how far they can stink up the country when them grapes are fermenting?"

"I've smelled it in California as well as France, Italy, and Switzerland," Terence laughed. "I like it. I think we'll all learn to like it."

It was clear that Fanny wanted a private conference with him, but he dodged her until Foster Bainbridge could be there. Foster had bought her the house she wanted in San Francisco. The bank would deposit fifteen hundred dollars to her checking account every quarter so long as she lived, married or unmarried.

"I'll never marry," she said, making up her mind to get it said whether or not Foster was there.

"Perhaps you're one of those one-man women for whom there is only one husband," Terence replied.

"I would have been happy with you," she said unblushingly.

"You only think so, Fanny. You're not cut out to be a cattleman's wife."

She looked around. They were sitting in the dining room at the end of the big table; María had announced that there was no sense in trying to change everything and that this room would stay as it was. "I've been happier here than I've been in years," she said. "It's a peaceful place, and you're a kind man." She stood up. "And I still mean that other. You know! You could have had both of us."

He shook his head. "It wouldn't work."

"It works all the time, all over California, all over México. It's too late to talk about it, but I just wanted you to know how I felt."

He thanked her; what else could he do?

Julia had accepted responsibility for Ernest, but he was causing her little trouble. She saw to his clothing and made him shave daily and bathe twice a week. She saw that he did not overeat but that he ate enough, too. Soon he would be eighty-nine, and his health was better than ever. He might be the one to reach one hundred years. Certainly in the dreamy, placid world in which he lived, there was nothing to disturb the serenity of his soul.

Ernest had adopted a dog that followed him everywhere except to the table; Julia would not stand for it being fed from his hand there. But it slept on a cushion beside his bed. It had its own place beside the circular bench around the pepper tree out back, and not even the chickens were permitted to take liberties there.

María and Eloísa were still upstairs with the maids, straightening out the new furniture in the master bedroom, when a rider came bearing important news.

Baron Godfrey had had cash enough hidden away to hire good lawyers, who got him a change of venue to Santa Barbara County. There he had been tried for the murders of the Viscainos, there being no way to convict him of Uncle Frank's murder. There just were no witnesses, nothing but hearsay.

Yesterday the jury had debated less than an hour before bringing in a verdict of guilty. The judge had immediately sentenced him to two death sentences. Baron had been ordered to rise to hear sentence pronounced. He tottered backward, screaming obscenities, and one of his lawyers caught him and kept him from falling.

They had to handcuff his one arm to a deputy's to get him out of the courtroom, still raving in fury, still convinced that life had cheated him out of money and wealth that was rightfully his.

From that moment on he talked of that old fool of a Frank McNeil, long past the time a man ought to die, sitting there in his goddamn chair on his goddamn porch and owning everything in sight. On the gallows he said, "Well, I took care of him, too! The old miser will never live to be a hundred now. One law for the rich and one for the poor. I fixed that old—"

He dropped to the end of the rope and was thenceforth silent forever.

But the word spread, and many a rider passing the Dot M Dot looked up at the big house and thought he could see a shadowy rocking chair with a loudmouthed, vindictive, overbearing old man in it, a man charged with constructive avarice as with gunpowder, sitting there and rocking as he counted what was his. And it *had* been his. The kind of man the times required had found him equal to every test.